BULLET FOR GOLD

Clint Jackson was doing what he did best—which was nothing—when he got his uncle's letter. He knew even before he opened it that the letter would spell trouble—and it sure as shootin' did! Clint's uncle Jeff, who had gone to Pine Creek, Colorado to stake a gold claim, was being roughed up and threatened by the notorious gunfighter Silk Barrister and his men. But Clint was a man to be reckoned with; he protected his own. Barrister and his gunnies had finally met their match when Clint arrived in the boom-town and staked a claim on their lives!

BULLET
FOR GOLD

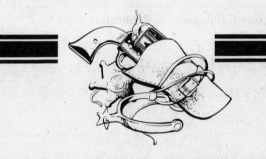

Dalton Loyd Williams

ATLANTIC LARGE PRINT
Chivers Press, Bath, England.
John Curley & Associates Inc.,
South Yarmouth, Mass., USA.

Library of Congress Cataloging in Publication Data

Williams, Dalton Loyd.
  Bullet for gold.

  (Atlantic large print)
  Published in large print.
  1. Large type books.   I. Title.
[PS3573.I44842B8   1985]   813'.54   84–14308
ISBN 0–89340–800–X

British Library Cataloguing in Publication Data

Williams, Dalton Loyd
  Bullet for gold.—Large print ed.—
  I. Title
  813'.54[F] PS3573.I4484/

  ISBN 0–7451–9009–X

This Large Print edition is published by Chivers Press, England, and
John Curley & Associates, Inc., U.S.A. 1985

Published by arrangement with Collier Associates

U.K. Hardback ISBN 0 7451 9009 X
U.S.A. Softback ISBN 0 89340 800 X

BULLET FOR GOLD

CHAPTER ONE

Clint Jackson rode through the rocky, walled mountain pass in the late evening twilight. He reined Star, his big roan horse, to a stop in the middle of the muddy wagon road. Then he sat loosely in the saddle overlooking the valley below him. After being on the trail for two weeks, the valley was a welcome sight.

At the upper end of the valley, gray misty sheets of rain filled the cool mountain air like a thin fog. Yet, even in the dimming light, Clint could still make out the large purple-green meadows of grass and the tall stands of aspen, oak, fir and pine trees which spread thickly across the valley floor and coated the surrounding slopes with a magical beauty.

At the foot of the mountain pass, Clint could see the raw mining town of Pine Creek, Colorado. The town was built along the winding wagon road and near the snow-fed stream it took its name from. Clint noticed that there were few trees in or around the town, or on the nearby slopes where the blackened openings of mine

1

shafts could be seen next to the dark shapes of log cabins.

The narrow stream that wound down the middle of the valley rushed out of the mountains through a jagged gash alongside the road. By looking down the dark crevice, Clint could see the black, foaming ribbon of water seventy feet below as it raced swiftly over the rocks on its long journey toward the sea.

Clint sat quietly in the saddle and studied the town. He saw the many tents, shacks, cabins, and buildings which had been hastily put up along the roadway and on the more level parts of the enclosing slopes. The yellowish glow of lanterns could be seen in front of the tents and buildings along the town's only street, and bits of light flickered through unchinked boards and tears in the canvas tents. Clint thought the town was an eyesore in such a peaceful-looking valley, but it was his destination.

All that afternoon, he'd ridden into a cold rain that was blowing out of the north, and the old, patched-up slicker he wore seemed to let in more water than it kept out. Clint had seen better days, but that old slicker had just about seen its last.

Clint had decided to push on for town,

even though Star was just about tuckered out from the long trip. Clint had never liked the idea of sleeping on the wet ground, not if he could avoid it, and since he was already cold and wet, he figured a few more hours in the saddle wouldn't matter too much one way or the other; especially when the difference would mean a hot meal and a warm bed to sleep in.

A man usually thinks about those comforts in his old age—although most folks wouldn't rightly consider thirty as being old. But if they happened to be a member of a homesteading family smack in the middle of Texas cow country, like Clint was, then they just might have some idea of why he considered thirty a ripe old age.

Down in Mason, Texas, most folks steered clear of the Jackson clan. Their status as homesteaders—the cattlemen usually called them 'damn nesters'—had made the Jacksons' social life a mite strained at times; in fact, most of the time. It also made the Jacksons clannish and sometimes downright scratchy; especially coming out of the mountains of North Carolina the way they did.

Mountain folks always tend to be clannish anyway, and the Jacksons more so

3

than most because their first loyalty was to the family. When it came to family, nothing else mattered. Right or wrong, good or bad, the family always came first.

Clint had always been pretty scratchy and a bit hard-headed himself, but he did have sense enough to get out of that Texas hill country when he was a youngster, even if it was just half a step ahead of a necktie party. If he had stayed around, the situation could have turned into a range war between the homesteaders and the cattlemen, and that's something any sane man tried to avoid.

The trouble had begun in the usual way. The cattlemen were complaining about the small herds of cows the homesteaders had built up. The ranchers claimed the homesteaders were getting their cows from the ranchers' unbranded stock, and since the big ranchers were rich and powerful, they had the law on their side most of the time.

Matters came to a head when Clint's pa, Jeremiah Jackson, discovered that some Jackson cows had been shot while grazing on free grass, which the ranchers claimed for their own.

Clint, being the hard-headed youngster

he was at the time, and a known hunter and tracker, set out a few old, rusty bear traps in retaliation. When old man Ernest Ramsey, the biggest rancher in the country, rode his prize Appaloosa into one of those traps and broke its leg, the warm-hearted ranchers decided to invite Clint to a little party.

Not being in a very sociable mood at the time, Clint decided to light a shuck out of the country. The far side of the Red River looked a whole lot healthier to him. Besides, he always had a yen to travel and that had looked like a good time to begin his journey.

Since those cattlemen were so warm-hearted, and since Clint was pretty quick when he had to be, they followed him all the way to the muddy Red hoping he might change his mind and join their little party, but they lost his trail in the river bottoms.

Once a man is branded with the Jackson iron, he's always a Jackson, and for that reason Clint was where he was at the moment: sitting on a big roan horse, wearing a leaky slicker, and getting colder by the minute while looking down at a mountain valley town called Pine Creek.

About two weeks earlier, things had been

different. Clint had been doing what he did best—nothing, and doing it for thirty dollars a month in a line shack in the Capulin Mountains of New Mexico. The line shack belonged to a rusty old he-coon named William Holden, but as far as that went, everything within seeing distance belonged to him. Holden had to be a pretty tough old coon with the times being what they were; it wasn't easy for a man to keep his life, much less his property. That's why Clint never had anything himself; he was always being too busy doing the first, to worry much about the second. The day to day problems of scratching for a living and staying alive were enough for him.

Anyhow, there he'd been, sitting up in the Capulin Mountains and just about as content as a man could ever hope to be. Spring was in the air after a winter of solitude, and the ice was beginning to melt. New grass was pushing up in the bare spots, and small animals were starting to stir after a long winter's sleep. Clint thought it was a fine time of the year to be alive.

That particular morning, he'd been standing outside the line shack stretching and watching some birds hunt for bugs in the new grass on the mountain slopes, while overhead, fleecy white clouds chased each other across the vast expanse of bright blue sky. Then he spotted old man Benjamin Dunton coming up the canyon with supplies to take his place at the line shack.

Clint was pleased to see the old man, more so since he'd run out of conversation with Star a month earlier. The big roan had taken to ignoring him during their conversations, and Clint could hardly get that hard-headed cayuse to say a word which made any sense. But it was old man Holden's policy to have only one man in the line shack during the winter. Two men together might get cabin fever and end up killing each other in frustration over a checker game. It had happened before.

Humming an off-key tune to himself, Clint put on a fresh pot of coffee to welcome the old man. He stoked the old potbellied stove so it would heat up quickly, then he took a seat on the doorstep. He lit a fresh stogie and could already taste the whisky he planned to drink in Los Alamos to wash the winter cobwebs out of his system.

But old man Dunton wasn't as happy

7

about seeing Clint as Clint was to see him. When Dunton rode into the yard, he had that sour look on his weather-beaten face that a man gets when he thinks about things like spending the whole summer riding line by himself, while his friends go into town every month and have a good time blowing their pay. It was enough to sour any man.

Clint felt sorry for the old man, but Dunton didn't appear to notice it because Clint just couldn't get that silly grin off his face long enough to set a proper mood.

After Dunton dismounted, they shook hands and settled themselves down in the cabin with a cup of hot coffee to take care of the necessary business of the cattle. Clint gave Dunton a head count, or as near as he could get, and filled him in on where the main groups of cows were holed up and what shape they were in after a winter in the canyons. With that business out of the way, Clint got up to help unload the two pack horses, but Dunton reached into his pocket and handed him a letter.

Even before he opened the letter, Clint knew it would spell trouble. Loose-footed men like him didn't get letters very often, and whenever they did, they usually ended up wishing they hadn't. The letter was the first one he'd gotten in years, so he sat down at the table and looked the envelope over carefully before opening it.

The letter had chased him just about all over the New Mexico Territory. It had been forwarded so much that he could hardly make out his name on it. But there it was, as big as all outdoors, Jefferson Clinton Jackson, so it had to be his since he didn't know of anyone with that brand. Outside of his name, a Fort Summer address, and the postage stamps, the envelope was blank, so he had to open it up to find out who'd written it.

The letter was over three months old and by the time he'd finished reading it—something which involved a lot of lip moving, frowning, and head scratching—he had something to think about.

It was from an uncle of his on his ma's side of the family who had managed to get his hands on a gold mine up at Pine Creek, Colorado. But now that he had struck pay-dirt, he was having a little trouble holding onto his claim. It seemed that some tough characters were trying to smoke him out, but so far the claim jumpers were having a mite of trouble.

9

Knowing his ma's family like he did, Clint realized his uncle wouldn't have ever written the letter unless things were pretty serious. Since his uncle was kinfolks, Clint thought he'd better get up there and take a hand in the ruckus. It wouldn't set well with his ma if he didn't, and Clint never liked to have his ma upset.

Just the thought of his ma brought a rare smile to Clint's lips. Even though she was a small woman, she had a lot of spirit, and men tended to walk a mite softly around her when she was upset. Even Clint's pa had been known to take to the hills, and he wasn't afraid of a mad grizzly.

'Yep,' Clint thought fondly, 'ma is a lot of woman and it would sure set bad with her if'n I didn't go try to help out Uncle Jeff with his troubles.'

Clint knew it meant he had a lot of riding to do, since Pine Creek was located in the high Rockies of Colorado, and he knew it would take a couple of weeks of hard riding to get up there.

He figured his uncle could hold out for another two weeks if he was still in possession of the mine, but he knew he had to hurry. Clint didn't have the slightest idea of what he would do when he got there, except maybe get himself shot; that idea had never appealed to him. Still, it was a family matter, and the Jacksons set a heap of store by the family.

After he had pondered the letter for a few minutes and made some tentative plans, Clint stuck the letter in his pocket and looked out the cabin door at old man Dunton with the thought that they might do some talking before he pulled out. But Clint saw that Dunton was in the middle of unloading the two pack horses, and from the grunts he made, along with the flushed expression on his face, Clint decided the very least he could do to help would be to saddle up and ride out, which would get him out of the old man's way.

Mounted on the roan, Clint waved to old man Dunton, who returned the favor by flashing Clint a sour look. Once away from the line shack, Clint made pretty good time all that day, and by late evening he arrived at the Big House to draw his pay.

William Holden's ranch was magnificent. Set close to a small, mountain-fed stream and encircled by rolling hills of grassland, the house was surrounded by tall cottonwoods. The house itself was one story with a high, peaked roof. It was built of tough adobe brick and was whitewashed with green trim around the windows. A large veranda extended across the front and was almost covered with morning glory vines, which bloomed in the spring and summer with a profusion of colors. The house was surrounded on three sides by out-buildings and corrals, and a large barn set well to the rear.

Clint collected his five months' pay, and he felt pretty rich carrying a hundred and fifty dollars in gold and silver coins in his poke. At any other time, he'd have pulled a two week drunk, but his Uncle Jeff needed him, so he knew he had to stay sober.

Since it was late in the day, he settled into the bunkhouse for the night, planning on getting an early start the next morning after having a big breakfast. According to plan, he drew some trail grub from the cook shack and was on his way north an hour before first light.

While riding the trail during the next two weeks, Clint had a lot of time to think, and he tried to remember everything he'd ever heard about his uncle, Jefferson Joshua Pickens. He'd never met Uncle Jeff himself, but he had heard some pretty hairy stories about Uncle Jeff's exploits from the time he'd been a runny-nose kid. From what he'd heard folks say, Uncle Jeff must have been a pretty salty old wolf in his younger days.

Uncle Jeff was one of the feuding Pickens clan out of the North Carolina mountains, and Clint had never met a Pickens who wasn't hard-headed and downright scratchy. He thought that that was where he'd gotten his own contrariness from, seeing as how he was half Pickens from his ma's side of the family.

The story that Clint remembered best about his uncle recounted the time he had gotten caught in the middle of the Snake River in the Northwest Territory by a bunch of Blackfeet Indians when he was trapping back in the beaver days.

Those young Blackfeet bucks had planned on having some sport with Uncle Jeff; not to mention the load of prime beaver pelts Uncle Jeff had in his bullboat, which those bucks had set their hearts on having. They thought of how Uncle Jeff's hair and those prime pelts would set them pretty high with the young squaws. And since there were a half dozen or so of them and only one Uncle Jeff, they didn't think there would be much argument about the matter.

But Uncle Jeff had other plans regarding his hair, which he'd gotten firmly attached to, and those pelts, which were worth a lot of money. So, being an unsociable old cuss, he spoiled their fun right off by killing two of them with his rifle and hatchet, then dumped the rest of them into the river by turning their canoe over with a push-pole.

Now, Blackfeet don't take too kindly to that sort of treatment, and seeing as how they had made such an effort to be sociable, for the next three days and nights it was touch and go whether or not Uncle Jeff was going to join those young bucks in the festivities they had planned for him. Uncle Jeff never did care much about being the guest of honor at an Injun shindig, but the Blackfeet tried to change his mind.

The evening of the third day, Uncle Jeff met a party of trappers, and those young bucks quickly decided they couldn't entertain so many white men at the same time in the style they were accustomed to.

Uncle Jeff sold those pelts and still had hair on his head as far as Clint knew. That was only one of the tells about him. There's a lot more stories, but most of them don't bear repeating; most especially when there's womenfolks around.

Thinking about the many tells he'd heard, Clint wondered if just maybe those varmints in Pine Creek hadn't taken on a mite more than they could handle. Then, having another member of the family take a hand in the goings-on sure wouldn't set well with those low-down crooks, and that was just what was going to happen.

Riding down the wagon road toward the muddy street running through the row of drab, rain-soaked tents and scattered buildings of the mining town, Clint looked it over carefully and was glad that the rain had finally stopped. Clint's pa had warned him that it always paid a man to size up an anthill before stomping on it; that is, if he doesn't plan on getting some of the little critters in his pants.

Clint knew there was no telling what he'd find in Pine Creek, but if it was anything like the other boom towns he had been in, then he knew it wouldn't be too pretty. He decided to be careful where he set his boots, so's not to get bit by some slimy snake while he was taking in the sights and sizing up the town.

He could see right off that as far as boom towns went, Pine Creek was as rip-roaring and wild as any of them. It had all the glittering attractions that a gold town could offer when money was plentiful, and Pine Creek appeared to have money to burn.

Almost overnight, mines like the Little Edna, Glory Hole, Fancy Nance, Sweet Lilly, and others had turned farmers and carpenters into millionaires as a stream of golden wealth poured from the ground in staggering amounts. Pine Creek would make a place for itself in the history books as one of the richest strikes in the Colorado Rockies. But from where Clint sat, it looked like the raw hell-hole it was.

Having ridden all that day from sunup and the last part of it in a cold rain, Clint was wet, cold, tired, and hungry when he entered town from the south. Touching spurs to the roan, he rode down the muddy street between the tent saloons, cribs, and gambling places that lined both sides of the street from one end of town to the other.

The only lights on the street came from smoky kerosene lanterns hanging on the fronts of the various businesses. In the darkening light, the lanterns cast a pale yellowish glow on the miners who stumbled on the muddy boards laid in front of and in between the tents and stores, and on the horses, mules, and donkeys that were tied to the hitching rails in front of the places.

All of this—the loud, raucous piano and banjo music, the high-pitched squeals of dance-hall girls, and the miners' drunken laughter from inside the saloons and cribs, spaced by an occasional gunshot and yell—wasn't the best reception for a man riding into town on serious business. But Clint knew from past experience that it was the best any boom town had to offer.

As he rode down the street, Clint did his best to keep the roan from stepping on a drunken miner who was lying almost invisible in the muddy street, while at the same time he searched for a place where he could get something to eat. Clint breathed a sigh of relief when he spotted a small sign hanging in front of a large tent with the legend: 'Joe's—Eat's—Drink's—Gambling.'

Most of the business establishments were tents and a few had wood siding added, except for the general store and assessment office, which were both built of logs. Where he ate didn't make any difference to him. Clint was so hungry that he could have eaten sitting in a mud puddle with a mad she-grizzly for company, so he turned the roan in at Joe's and stopped before the pine-post hitching rail, then dismounted slowly. Having been in the saddle so long, he felt like every joint in his body was glued in its socket.

CHAPTER TWO

Clint stomped around in the mud for a minute to get his blood circulating, then loosened the cinch on the saddle so the roan could breathe a little easier. Taking off his slicker, he laid it across the saddle in case it rained while he was inside.

It never failed to make Clint's blood boil when he saw some greenhorn leave a horse standing for hours cinched up tighter than a diamond hitch. He thought a man didn't deserve to own a horse if he didn't know how to take care of it. Still, it was mighty hard for Clint to look the roan in the eyes after leaving him tied to the hitching rail like that, especially since he was looking forward to a bucket of oats and a dry stall for himself. But Clint hadn't seen any sign of a livery stable on the way in, and he didn't have the slightest idea of how long he'd be in town, or how quickly he might have to leave.

When he stepped inside the tent, Clint wasn't expecting all the sudden attention he got. The loud talking died down almost instantly. Everyone turned to look at him as though they were trying to decide whether the cat had dragged him in or if he'd made it under his own power.

Being alone so much, Clint hadn't paid much attention to his appearance, but to the miners, he must have looked a sight. He was a big man anyway. Clint stood a couple of inches over six feet without his boots, and weighed over two hundred pounds, most of which was in his chest and shoulders. That alone was usually enough to get him unwarranted attention when he was around city folks.

Clint knew it couldn't have been his smell that attracted those miners' attention, because even though he hadn't seen a bar of soap in over four months, the stink inside the tent told him that neither had the miners.

He thought it might be the way he dressed. The Texas flat-crown hat he wore sagged down in front and back from the rain, but did little to hide the long thick

19

mane of black hair, which hadn't been trimmed in over a year. It could have been his high-heeled cowman's boots with the big Spanish rowels that jingled when he walked, because everybody else seemed to be wearing flat-heeled, logging type boots that laced up to mid-shin with pants tucked into the tops.

Clint stood in the doorway of the tent in his worn range clothes and scratched his heavy winter beard until the miners and the others went to talking again and minding their own business. Then he headed for an empty table he'd spotted at the back of the tent.

The inside of the tent was about thirty feet long and twenty feet wide, and had a hard-packed dirt floor. On one side, a pine-plank bar that sat on empty beer kegs ran the full length of the tent, and there were several tables scattered around for eating, drinking, and gambling. In the center of the tent stood a potbellied stove with a fire glowing inside that drove out the damp chill and filled the tent with a snug warmth. The interior was lit by four hanging lanterns that cast a yellowish glow and gave a shadowy effect to the corners of the tent, along with giving out the pungent odor of kerosene.

After reaching the table he wanted, Clint opened the buttons of his sheepskin coat and sank into the chair. He placed his back against the canvas wall so he could keep an eye on everything inside the tent and look the customers over at the same time.

Five men were bellied up to the bar on his right and a dozen or more were scattered around the tent eating and drinking at the tables. A couple of serious card games were going on at the tables directly beneath the hanging lanterns. Clint saw that most of the men wore rough miner's garb; flat-heeled boots, corduroy pants, wool shirts, wide leather belts with pistol or knife scabbards hanging from them, and wool jackets or coats. Most of the miners had shed their coats in the warmth of the tent.

After a short wait, a fat, red-faced man wearing a greasy leather apron came out from the back of the tent and walked over to where Clint was sitting. He stood wiping his meaty hands on a dirty, once-white towel.

'Can I help you, Mister?' The fat man asked gruffly, as though he could have cared less.

'Yep, I reckon so,' Clint replied slowly, while he looked the man over and didn't like what he saw. The rolls of fat hung on him like slabs of tallow and a rank, unwashed odor seemed to float about him like a cloud of flies. 'What've you got in the line of grub?'

'There's beans or stew, three dollars a bowl. Sourdough biscuits, four bits each. And coffee, two bits a cup. Pay in advance,' the fat man replied, while he eyed Clint's worn range clothes appraisingly and instantly dismissed him as a saddle tramp and a drifter.

Digesting the information about the food, Clint wasn't surprised at the high prices. All mining towns imported everything by mule train, then, when roads were built, by freight wagons, which made prices go sky high. But three dollars for a bowl of beans was outrageous.

'Friend, don't you think that's a mite steep for groceries?' Clint asked in a reasonable tone of voice.

The fat man curled his upper lip in a sneer, then, with unmistakable contempt in his voice, he said: 'Look, Mister, you want to eat or not? I've got better things to do, so take it or leave it. I'm not needin' your business that bad.'

Clint could clearly see the fat man needed knocking off the high horse he was riding. He didn't want to pay that much for a meal, but then, he didn't want to leave without eating. Figuring the prices would be about the same anywhere else, he ordered the beans—since stews were chancy things, and there was no telling what the fat man would put into it—biscuits and coffee.

With reluctance, he watched the fat man carry his hard-earned dollars into the kitchen. Clint also noticed that the men in the tent had been watching the exchange and were grinning to each other like they shared a special joke which he couldn't quite see or understand.

Giving no heed to their grins, Clint dug into the bowl of beans the fat man brought him and tried to forget how much each mouthful was costing him. At the same time, he kept his eyes glued to the rest of the men in the tent; especially two of the men at the bar, because they were acting a little livelier than the rest.

One of them was a big, burly man, several inches taller than Clint, and a good forty pounds heavier. He was wearing miner's clothes and had a big bowie knife hanging from his belt in a fringed scabbard, but he wore no gun that Clint could see. The man had a bearded face which reminded Clint of an old horned bull he had roped down in Texas, and Clint immediately thought of him as Bullface.

The man beside him, who appeared to be his friend, was a lot shorter and lighter; skinny looking, even in the bulky coat he wore. His face was sharp, with a long, thin nose and constantly shifting, dark, beady eyes. His long brown hair looked stringy and greasy, as though it hadn't been washed in a long time. From the way he kept scratching his head, Clint would have bet his last dollar that the man had plenty of company in the brown, greasy mop of hair. The thin man was wearing a strangely long, knee-length coat which was unbuttoned down the front. Taken totally, the man reminded Clint of a weasel.

Behind the long bar, there was a young redheaded girl of sixteen or seventeen, who was tending to the drinking customers. She was a pretty sight, with a sprinkle of tiny brown freckles across her pert little nose and cheeks, and with thick red hair that flowed over her shoulders like a river of silk. She looked very pretty in the blue gingham dress that was trimmed with white lace.

With her behind the bar was a thin, redheaded, freckle-faced boy of eleven or twelve, who was washing glasses in a bucket of water. At least he was trying to wash them. Those two men who'd captured Clint's attention were having a lot of fun giving both of the youngsters a hard time.

A few choice phrases drifted back to Clint's ears and caused his temper to rise, because Bullface seemed to be speaking for the whole tent's benefit.

'Hey, boy, do a better job on 'em glasses,' Bullface taunted with an ugly sneer. 'I can see the dirt from here. How'd you like to drink outta a glass like that? Boy, you tryin' to give me the runs?' he said loudly. Then, turning to the fat man, he said: 'Joe, you gonna pay that brat for sloppy work like that? It appears to me he oughtta be payin' you!'

Bullface watched the girl move back and forth behind the bar serving the customers, then he said leeringly: 'Hey little girl, is it true what they say 'bout redheaded gals?'

The girl ignored him like he was a pile of horse manure and turned up her small nose

25

in utter distaste. But Bullface wasn't abashed and continued in an even louder tone of voice.

'Now, I've always heard tell that redheaded gals got red hair all over. So how 'about it gal? You got red hair all over?' he demanded, then laughed loudly, as did the weasel-faced man in a high falsetto.

The girl turned a beet red with shame, which hid her freckles, and the boy's ears turned red with embarrassment. To Clint, they looked as if they were sister and brother, and he tightened his jaw in anger. It was up to the owner of the place to stop the man, but he didn't. Rather, he appeared to be real chummy with the two polecats who were baiting the kids, and Clint could plainly see that the fat man wasn't about to do or say anything that might spoil their fun.

What happened next probably wouldn't have happened if Clint hadn't been as tired as he was, and still somewhat mad about the high price of the meal he was eating. But then, Clint just naturally didn't like bullies anyway, and those two were beginning to get under his skin with their loud, coarse talk around those youngsters.

Down in Texas, men treated womenfolks

and kids with a kind of gentleness, them being so weak and all; or else a man just might end up on the wrong end of a bull-whip, or maybe the singing end of a rope from the nearest tree. But those two jaspers didn't appear to have been brought up proper at all. As Clint raised the cup of two-bit coffee to his lips to take another sip, Bullface made a serious mistake and the weasel cheered him on like the slimy snake he was.

With a leering smirk on his beefy face that revealed ugly, yellow-stained teeth, Bullface waited until the girl had moved within reach of him to serve one of the other customers. Then, with a lunge, he quickly reached out, grabbed her by the arm and dragged her halfway across the bar.

The girl uttered a surprised, frightened cry and her face turned a chalky white, which made her freckles stand out across her cute nose and cheeks. Then with silent determination, she began to struggle to get free of the huge hand that was holding her so tightly.

At the same time, the boy turned around furiously and tried to come to her rescue as he yelled: 'Leave my sister alone!' Then he

27

slipped through the beer kegs that supported the bar top and threw himself against the big man's knees.

The boy looked like a badger attacking a grizzly bear. He had plenty of heart, but not enough size, so it was a gallant yet futile effort. With his free hand, Bullface grabbed the boy by the hair, bent him down and delivered a hard kick to the boy's posterior. The kick sent him flying back under the bar and into the glass rack, upending it and sending glasses crashing to the dirt floor. The boy lay still for several seconds, then he got shakily to his feet, a small trickle of blood oozing from a fresh cut over his eye.

'Mind your manners, you young brat!' Bullface said in a deep growl. 'Me and your pretty sister is gonna get acquainted, ain't we gal?' he leered with an ugly grin.

The weasel began to laugh excitedly while the girl's face twisted in pain and revulsion. The other men in the tent chose to either ignore what was happening to the kids, or else look shame-faced about not trying to put a stop to the ruckus.

It appeared to Clint that the two bullies had everybody in the place buffaloed, and he knew right then that he wasn't going to finish eating his high-priced meal. That made him feel downright sad since he'd already paid for it. But there were some things Clint just couldn't tolerate, and Bullface had made a serious mistake, maybe a fatal one.

The girl's eyes searched the tent for someone to help her, and at the same time she continued her silent struggle in an attempt to free herself from the man's iron grip. But it seemed to Clint that all the men were afraid of the two bullies who were making the girl's life so miserable, and she was completely on her own with nothing but her own courage to help her.

Clint set his coffee cup down on the table just as Bullface started to wrap his other arm around the girl to lift her over the bar. Clint could see that she was hanging onto the edge of the bar for dear life, while trying to twist out of Bullface's grip. Then Clint spoke, keeping his voice low and soft.

'Leave her be,' Clint said, and saw Bullface's hand stop in mid-air.

Everybody in the tent heard Clint's words, even though they'd been spoken low. The weasel's shrill laughter suddenly died out on a high note and everything in the tent got deathly quiet. The only sounds that could be heard were the crackling of the fire in the potbellied stove and the heavy breathing of the girl as she continued her desperate struggles to free herself.

Clint held a considerable advantage, sitting in the shadows. He was slightly behind Bullface and the man had to turn almost completely around to see him. But even then, Bullface couldn't see his face because of the hat brim pulled down, almost hiding his eyes, and because of his heavy winter beard.

For a span of about thirty seconds, Bullface just looked and Clint used the time to loosen the pistol in his holster and to take a log black cigar out of his shirt pocket. He struck a match with the thumbnail of his left hand as his right hand rested near the pistol.

'Mister, maybe you've got a hearin' problem,' he said in the same low, clear voice. 'I said, leave her be!'

Every town has its own bully, and Bullface seemed to be the king-of-the-walk in Pine Creek. Evidently he thought he was about as mean as barbed wire. Clint could tell that Bullface wasn't about to get put down in front of all the townfolks by a nameless, unknown saddle tramp, and

Bullface confirmed it as soon as he got over the shock of Clint's challenging words.

'You got a rock between your ears, cowboy?' Bullface demanded in a sneering voice. Then holding up his huge, hamlike fist, he waved it in the air at Clint and continued talking in a deep growl: "Cause if'n you do, I've got a stamp-mill here that'll sure knock it loose.'

The weasel snickered and slapped the bar-top with the flat of his hand as though it was the funniest thing he had ever heard in all his natural born life. Then someone else in the tent giggled expectantly, as if on cue.

Seeing that he had everyone's attention, Bullface glared challengingly at Clint as he continued to hold the struggling girl.

'You just mind your own business, cowboy, and get outta here a'fore I throw you out,' he bellowed, and continued to shake his huge fist in the air at Clint.

Clint could see that everyone was just itching to see a good fight. Excitement seemed to hang in the air and the men shifted to get a better view, or else stood up along the canvas walls of the tent as they moved back out of the way. It appeared that none of them thought Clint's chances were too good, but then, they didn't know him either.

Jacksons learned how to fight even before they learned to walk, and they didn't fight for fun either, they fought to win. Clint had been winning fights for so long that he couldn't even remember the last time he'd gotten whipped, although he'd fought to a draw a few times.

To look at Bullface, a man would have thought that he had the fight already won, and he didn't expect much trouble from the drifting cowboy. But like most bullies, he wanted to talk it up a little more first, which he thought would give him some kind of an advantage over Clint, who was just sitting there at the table nice and easy, inspecting his cigar. Then, before Bullface could say something else, Clint spoke again.

'Mister, the way I see it,' he spoke in the same low, soft voice, 'a man that don't have any respect for womenfolks couldn't have been raised proper. His ma must've spent most of her time under the back porch scratchin' fleas. Of course, you could be half snake, but it's kind'a early in the year for the slimy things to be out, so I'm kind'a wonderin' which brand fits a low-down coward like you.'

For several moments Bullface stared at Clint, not believing his ears. From the way his face turned purple, a man would have thought he was about to bust a gut. Like flicking off a pesty fly, he flung the girl from his hand. She flew backward with a small cry of surprise, and rubbed her bruised arm when she regained her balance. Then, with a roar of rage, Bullface charged across the tent at Clint with his arms held wide like an angry bear about to close in on a man and crush the life out of him.

When Clint had sat down at the table, he'd noticed that the wood box for the stove was next to his table. It was setting against the canvas wall beside his chair. He stuck the cigar in his mouth and waited until the charging bully had almost reached him, then Clint swiftly reached down and closed his hand around a piece of firewood about the same size as his arm and about eighteen inches long.

Just as Bullface was almost on top of him, Clint came up from under the table with the length of firewood and jammed it right into Bullface's stomach with all his strength. He made a direct hit in the man's solar plexus, just as a hamlike fist began a roundhouse swing which died out as quickly as the breath that exploded from the man's lungs.

Bullface stopped dead in his tracks, as though he had run into an oak tree. His mouth dropped open with surprised pain and his eyes nearly popped out of his head. Then his knees buckled as his face turned a pasty white above the heavy beard. Bullface leaned sickly on the table with one hand for support and held his middle with the other hand. All the fight was suddenly gone out of him.

With a calm sureness, Clint rose to his feet and grabbed a handful of the man's hair securely in his fist, then slammed the beefy face into the top of the heavy oak table with a sharp splat.

Keeping a tight grip on the hair to prevent Bullface from sliding to the floor, Clint took the cigar out of his mouth and blew the ashes from the tip until it glowed a cherry red. Then with a cold contempt, he crammed the live cigar into Bullface's ear and twisted it off.

A bellowing scream tore from Bullface's throat and Clint shoved him contemptuously to the floor, where he thrashed about like a snake being beaten with a stick, while he continued to bellow screams of pain.

Out of the corner of his eye, Clint saw the weasel whip up the twin barrels of a very deadly looking .12 gauge, sawed-off shotgun from under the long coat he was wearing, while the thin, sharp features of his face twisted in ugly hatred.

Although Clint was no gunfighter, he had been born into a family that took an uncommon interest in weapons, so he'd had plenty of experience in handling one, and could get his out of the holster pretty quickly when the need arose.

Whirling and stepping to one side at the same time, he drew, cocked the pistol as it left the holster, and fired in one smooth, fluid-like motion. The forty-four caliber Remington made a crashing roar in the confines of the tent and belched a foot of flame from the blue steel barrel.

The first bullet caught the weasel in the shoulder, twisting him away from the bar by the heavy impact, and the second bullet, seemingly less than an instant later, caught him lower down in the right side of the chest. At the same time, both barrels of the Greener exploded with a deafening roar.

The twin loads of horseshoe nails blasted the door off the potbellied stove and blew a shower of hot coals all over the tent, while the weasel crumpled to the floor.

Clint's ears were still ringing from all the deafening shots when he recocked the heavy pistol, its four deadly clicks giving a warning to whoever could still hear, and most especially a warning to the fat owner of the tent, whose hands had disappeared under the bar top. Like he was about to get snake bite, the fat man froze and stared across the room into the big, dark bore of the forty-four that was leveled between his eyes.

'Fat man, don't do somethin' that you won't live to tell 'bout,' Clint drawled in a cold voice that carried to every corner of the tent. 'Now, why don't you just put both of your fat paws up on the bar top where I can see 'em a'fore I get excited and decide to ventilate that lard belly of yours.'

Clint looked anything but excited. In fact, the look on his face showed nothing except serious business and a calm readiness to squeeze the trigger of the cannon he held steadily in his hand.

With fear in his eyes, the fat man slowly brought his hands from under the counter and lay them on the top of the bar. The experience of looking into those cold, gray eyes and the black bore of the forty-four revolver had made his knees go weak and trembly with fear. Life suddenly seemed very precious to him and he knew positively that he'd been a heartbeat away from death.

Sweeping the tent with his eyes, Clint saw that the weasel was lying stretched out on the floor in front of the bar and was still alive, but he was breathing raspingly and was unconscious. Bullface was sitting on the dirt floor holding his head with both hands as he sobbed and rocked back and forth in pain. He had forgotten everybody else in the tent in his misery.

All the other men had backed up against the canvas walls of the tent or had hit the floor when the shooting started and were just now beginning to get back to their feet. None of the men made any hostile moves, appearing to want no part of the ruckus.

Seeing that the situation was under control, Clint glanced over at the redheaded boy and his sister who were standing behind the bar. Both youngsters were looking at him and the scene of total destruction with wide eyes and awed expressions on their faces. The boy's blue eyes stared with wonderous fascination at the big forty-four in Clint's hands. He'd never seen a gun drawn so fast or such destruction in so short a period of time. The girl stared at him with a mixture of fear and hero worship for what he'd done to save her.

Clint spoke quietly to the youngsters and watched everybody in the tent at the same time: 'I don't know why you two kids are workin' here, but I think maybe somethin' else can be found to beat this. So if you want to leave, you can both come with me right now.'

'They ain't a'goin' nowhere!' the fat man protested hotly, his face turning ugly at the thought of losing such cheap labor in the high-priced mining town.

'Mister,' Clint drawled slowly, as he gave the fat man a cold look, 'you just keep your trap shut and leave 'em paws of yours on the bar, and we'll get along mighty fine. These kids will do their own decidin'.'

He could see that both of the youngsters were scared, maybe more of him than what they'd just been through, but they had spunk and instantly decided to trust him. After all, he'd been the only one who'd helped them.

The girl pursed her lips and squared her small shoulders with determination as she peeled off the apron. Then, taking her brother by the arm, she led him out from behind the bar and stood looking at Clint for a moment.

'We're ready, mister, and glad we'll be to shake the dust of this vile place from our feet,' she said in a girlish voice, which was high and clear, and had a pleasant Irish lilt to it. Her voice was full of determination, which matched the stubborn look of pride on her pretty face and flashing green eyes.

Turning to the fat man, Clint said softly and evenly: 'If you're owin' these kids wages, don't you think you ought to be payin' 'em?' Although it was a question, there was no mistake that the words conveyed a command.

'Who's gonna pay for 'em busted glasses?' The fat man whined.

'That's your problem, mister,' Clint said without interest, adding: 'I don't know and I don't rightly care. I just reckon you'll have to raise the price on that stinkin' slop you serve. Now, I've asked you real friendly-like for their wages, so don't make me take it outta your greasy hide.'

While the fat man paid the kids, scowling while he did it, Clint watched the other men in the tent and kept them covered with the forty-four Remington. But none of the men seemed overly anxious to get mixed up in the scrape or tangle with the bearded cowboy.

It appeared that Bullface was going to have a hearing problem for sure now, and the weasel looked like he was getting ready to cash in his chips at any moment. He was conscious now and coughing blood, which is a mighty bad sign for a man with a chest wound. Clint looked at him without sympathy and figured that the bullet had gotten him in the lungs.

After the youngsters had collected their pay, Clint had them scoot on out the tent door while he guarded their exit. Then he moved carefully through the tent, so as not to turn his back on anyone. Just as he reached the door, the fat man decided to get mouthy again.

'Mister,' he said, his dark eyes blazing with hatred, 'I don't know who you are, but you're gonna regret the day you ever seen Pine Creek. I'll see to that.'

Clint studied the fat man with contempt and said icily: 'Fat man, you might see to it, but you sure can't handle the job yourself. For now, why don't you button those fat lips a'fore I get tired of hearin' all that hot air blowin' around.'

He then swept the tent once more with a cold look and said in his low, soft voice of steel: 'Gents, I'm leavin' now and if'n any of you got any fool notions like those two varmints on the floor, I'll be more'n glad to oblige you just like I did 'em. There won't be nothin' outside this door for you except hot lead. It might pay you to remember that!'

While the men stood scowling or looking sheepish, they saw the coldness in his gray eyes and would remember that look long after the words he spoke were forgotten. Clint then stepped backward through the tent flap to join the two kids who were waiting for him.

CHAPTER THREE

Outside the tent, Clint didn't waste any time untying the roan and leading him around to the side of the tent where they would be in the darkness. He saw that the worn slicker he'd left lying over the saddle was gone. Some lowdown skunk had stolen it while he'd been inside, and he hoped the thieving polecat never crossed his trail while wearing it.

Once they were in the shadows, Clint flipped open the cylinder of the pistol, and with deft movements he shucked out the two spent casings, then replaced them and added a third, which was something he rarely did. Usually, he kept the chamber under the hammer empty.

Wasting as little time as possible, he quickly tightened the cinch strap and mounted the roan. Then, reaching down, he lifted the girl and placed her sidesaddle in front of him, and was surprised at how light she was. As he reined out toward the street, he kicked his foot out of the stirrup and helped the boy swing up behind him.

The boy's hands fastened themselves onto the back of his gunbelt and he held the girl secure in his right arm, feeling her firm flesh under the thin fabric of her dress. She surrendered to the situation, leaning against his chest and gripping the roan's mane with her right hand and holding Clint's arm with her left.

Star didn't take kindly to all the extra

weight and the rustling of skirts, so he laid back his ears and gave a snort to express his feelings, which was something he'd been trained to never do. Then he hunched the muscles of his back as he gave considerable thought to dumping them all into the muddy street.

Clint was the only one who had ever rode him, having raised him from a colt, and carrying double—much less triple—was something Star just wasn't used to. Besides, he was tired and a little put out about the absence of a dry stall and a ration of grain. Clint knew what was going through the roan's mind, and gave him a touch of the spurs to give him something else to think about, while Clint gave some thought to their present situation.

He just couldn't understand what caused him to get into such predicaments, but he seemed to have a talent for such things. Now he was stuck with a girl and a boy who he knew nothing about, except that they needed help. For all he knew, a posse might get on his trail at any minute for kidnapping, and the last thing in the world he wanted was to be the guest of honor at another necktie party. The possibilities of it made Clint feel mighty uncomfortable.

So far, neither of the kids had said anything, and Clint could feel the girl begin to shiver from the cold air. With a start, he realized that the clean smell of the girl's hair wasn't simply soap, but a trace of perfume, more like a grown woman would use.

It would have helped if he could have let her wrap his slicker around her shoulders, but it was gone now and not worth worrying about. He hoped that whoever the polecat was that stole it needed it bad. The only thing Clint could do at the moment was to open his coat and let her snuggle into it the best she could.

'Thank you,' she said softly as he wrapped it clumsily around her shoulders.

She could smell his unwashed odor and feel the heavy beard brush against her hair, but none of that mattered to her. He was like a knight in shining armor for coming to her rescue. Not even knowing where he was taking her, she was unafraid and content as she leaned quietly against his broad chest.

Clint knew the boy sitting in back of him was as bad off as the girl in front, and he was going to have to figure out what to do with them. So Clint decided that he'd better find out something about the kids.

'You kids got names?' Clint asked.

'Yes,' the girl answered quickly, 'I'm Mary McDonald and my brother's name is Kevin. May I ask who you are, and where are you taking us?'

Mary's voice had that clear Irish lilt to it, not very strong, but still detectable. Like most Irish men and women, it had the firm ring of determination and pride in it, and her words fell pleasantly about his ears like soft music.

'Well, missy, my handle is Jefferson Clinton Jackson, but I mostly answer to the name of Clint, since Jefferson is a mighty big mouthful to say. Besides, I've got an uncle that calls himself Jeff. I ain't got the slightest idea of where I'm goin' to take you and your brother, or what I'm goin' to do with you when I get there. Right now, missy, I'm lookin' for a livery stable, so that'll do for a start.'

'Mr. Jackson, you may call me Mary. I am not at all sure that I like being called missy very much,' she informed him pertly. 'The stables are further down the street where we have our wagon. You don't have to concern yourself about my brother and me, though we thank you kindly for your help back there. But, Mr. Jackson, we don't want charity, so we will say good-by at the stables and be thanking you then.'

She sounded so prideful and determined that it made Clint feel that life must have dealt her some hurts along the way, so he replied quietly: 'Well, missy, I ain't offerin' any charity, and if'n you don't mind, I'd just as soon not be called "mister" like that, even if I'm older'n you. It kind'a sticks in my ear sockets. Missy, if'n you'll tell me how I can get you to your kinfolks, then I'll see you and your brother get to 'em safe and sound. You've got an important thin' to learn. There's a bit of difference between charity and lendin' a hand where it's needed. Most folks out here learn to tell the difference.'

Up until now the boy had let his sister do all the talking for both of them, but now he spoke up and the Irish lilt was more distinctive in his young voice. 'We ain't got no kinfolks, Clint, at least not around here. Ma and Pa died two weeks ago from fever. We still have our wagon and team at the livery, so if you will take us there, we'll be all right,' he said with more confidence than he actually felt.

Mary and Kevin McDonald were first

generation Irish-Americans, their parents having immigrated to America nearly twenty years before. The family had been heading for the cheap lands in the west determined to make a home for themselves away from the hostile discrimination that the Irish suffered in the cities of the east.

When their father, John McDonald, heard about the gold strike in Pine Creek, he'd turned aside with the hope of striking it rich before continuing on west. But he and his wife, Colleen, had contracted the deadly cholera shortly after arriving in town and died, leaving Mary and Kevin orphans in a hostile land.

Afraid that the authorities would put them into an orphanage, or separate them, Mary convinced Kevin to swear that she was eighteen if anybody asked. But Pine Creek was a booming gold town with everyone interested only in getting rich, so no one had bothered to ask—or seemed to care—what happened to two 'Micks', even if they were just kids.

Clint knew that they were trying to keep up a brave front, but he could see through their words. Underneath their stubbornness and pride, they were just a couple of scared kids who had been tossed haphazardly into an uncaring world. Clint hated to think of what the girl would end up having to do just so she and her brother could survive if nobody gave them a helping hand. Mary wouldn't be the first young girl to end up in a crib, because boom towns just don't offer choices; at least not to women.

Towns like Pine Creek were always full of men like Bullface and the weasel. There were plenty of desperados, saloon thugs, back-shooters, and similar scum who didn't have an ounce of mercy or goodness in their hearts for anyone except themselves. In the beginning of every boom town, it was always the rougher elements who held the upper hand until the good men finally stood up to the scum and formed vigilante groups to rid themselves of such men.

Clint knew that if he hadn't interfered back there at Joe's, it was no telling how far Bullface might have gone with the friendless girl. Maybe even forcing her to submit to his lust and leaving her no choice when it was over, except to become a crib girl. A woman didn't have a chance in a mining town unless she had money, or was respectably married.

Whatever happened now, and as much as

he didn't want to admit it, Clint knew that he was responsible for the two youngsters, because there wasn't anyone else they could turn to. It gave Clint a strange feeling, for up until now, the only things he'd been responsible for were his own hide and Star. The thought of having someone else to look out for made him feel mighty uncomfortable.

The roan plodded down the muddy street until the livery stable appeared near the edge of town. It was one of the few permanent buildings of Pine Creek, and was built of weathered one-by-twelve planks set vertically with weather strips nailed over the cracks.

Its design followed that of most stables in the west at the time. It had a high, false front, with a corral at one side and the back, and a wagon yard on the other side. One of the large double doors in front was standing open, and the interior was dimly lit by a kerosene lantern.

Clint rode directly into the stable through the open door, not surprised that the stable was floored, even though it was higher than the street, and therefore was dry inside. At the rear was another large double door, but it was closed to keep out the cold wind. Stalls ran down both sides of the walls, and a few nickers and snorts called out a greeting to Star.

Clint didn't see the hostler, so he helped the girl down and the boy quickly slipped off by himself. Then Clint dismounted, and the hostler came out of a small tackroom set at the front corner of the building.

'Howdy stranger,' the old hostler said from the gloom, 'think it'll rain?' Then, seeing the kids, he added sharply: 'Mary, Kevin, what've you youngsters been up to?'

'Nothing, Mr. Tollett,' Kevin said quickly.

Turning around, Clint saw the whiskered, dried-up-looking old man who walked with a limp. The old man was staring at him and the two kids from under bushy eyebrows with eagle-sharp eyes that were as clear and bright as amber beads.

'It might if'n it'll cloud up a mite,' Clint replied in a quiet voice, then asked: 'What's the price of a stall and feed for my horse, and maybe some information?'

The old man regarded him suspiciously for a moment, then turning his head slightly, he spit a long, brown stream of tobacco juice into a pile of dirty straw near the door, and said evenly: 'Stall's a dollar a night, feed's a dollar more. I don't sell information, stranger. Anythin' else?'

Clint saw that the hostler was a grumpy old buzzard, but if anyone in town would know about Uncle Jeff Pickens, it was bound to be him. Sooner or later, everyone in town who owned a horse or mule could be found at the livery stable. If there was any horse doctoring, shoeing, or buying and selling of horses, it was usually done through the hostler, or by him.

Also, during the day, most of the do-nothings around town used the stables as a kind of hang-out where they chewed tobacco, gossiped, and told stories. That always made the hostler a man worth knowing in any town in the west, especially if you needed information.

'I'd like to stall and feed my horse,' Clint said. 'He surely is tired. But a'fore I unsaddle, I have to know where I can find an old man by the name of Jeff Pickens. He owns a mine called the Sweet Lady somewhere here 'bouts.'

The hostler's eyes narrowed sharply as soon as Clint mentioned his uncle's name, then he looked from Clint to the youngsters and back again as he asked sharply:

'Mister, who're you working for? Wouldn't be Silk Barrister by any chance, would it?'

The old man's voice was raspy and full of suspicion as he continued to eye Clint sharply. Clint had heard of Silk Barrister, and knew if he was in town, then it sure wasn't to minister to the sick, or build any churches.

In every gold town there were always gamblers, conmen, cutthroats, and gunslicks. But men like Silk Barrister were a breed all their own. His kind would wait until a mining claim proved up, then he moved in. If the owner couldn't be bought out cheap, cheated at cards, or scared off, then the miner usually disappeared, or had a fatal accident of some kind, like lead poisoning in the back. Then Silk Barrister, or someone like him, would produce a bill of sale, partnership papers, or an IOU, which would give him the right to move onto the claim.

With a glimmering of what the old man was thinking, Clint realized that no information would be forthcoming, so he said: 'No, I ain't workin' for Silk Barrister. I've heard of him though, and the last I heard he was in Carson City.'

'Too bad he didn't stay there,' the old

man said with a snort. 'Instead, he brought his mischief here. What're you wantin' with old Jeff?'

Instead of answering the question, Clint pulled out the letter and handed it to the old hostler. He took it and limped over to the lantern, then held it up to the light and looked it over for a moment. Not even bothering to open it, he brought it back and handed it to Clint.

'So you're the nephew that Jeff told me 'bout. You could've said so straight out,' the old man said reproachfully, while he gave Clint a closer inspection, noting the worn pistol hanging on the cartridge belt. 'What're you doing with these two youngsters?' he demanded sharply.

Clint explained briefly what had happened up the street at Joe's, and when he finished, the old man scratched the gray stubble on his chin and looked steadily at Clint for a moment.

'Youngsters, you back up what he says?' the old man asked, and Mary and Kevin both nodded their heads. 'Okay, I'm satisfied.'

Then holding out his hand, he said: 'Mark Tollett's my handle, Clint, if'n you don't mind me callin' you that.'

'I'd rather you did,' Clint replied, taking the proffered hand and pumping it several times. 'One Jeff in the family at a time is enough.'

''Specially an old he-coon like your Uncle Jeff. But he was kind'a put out when you went to usin' your middle name,' Mark said with a chuckle.

'How do you know?' Clint asked curiously.

'Your uncle's a friend of mine, Clint. Been knowin' him for a coon's age. That's why I was a mite suspicious, but you'll see why when I tell you what you've gotten yourself into here,' Mark said. Then, looking at the youngsters, he added: 'That was right decent of you doin' what you done for these hard-headed youngsters. Ain't many around here right now that would've done it.' Then, speaking sternly to the kids, he said: 'I told you 'bout workin' at that place. Hard-headed Micks can't take advice if your lives depended on it. Well, I hope you've learned somethin' outta this. Did you?'

'Yes, sir,' Kevin answered in a small voice, but Mary raised her chin defiantly and returned his look with flashing eyes as she squared her shoulders with

54

stubbornness.

'Mark, if'n you'll tell 'bout Uncle Jeff, I'd be obliged,' Clint said to take the old man's attention off the kids, who he could see didn't like being lectured. 'But right now, I'd like to get my horse taken care of. He's a mite wore out.'

'I'll do it for you, Clint,' Kevin said quickly. Not waiting for permission, he took up the reins and led the roan toward a nearby stall.

'I'll help,' Mary said, and followed her brother.

'Heh, heh,' Mark chuckled, and said: 'Couple of nice kids there, but stubborn as mules. I'm keeping their team and wagon for 'em 'til they get a stake together.' Then, remembering Clint, he added: 'Come on in the office, and I'll give you the goods on 'em two you tangled with at Joe's, and 'bout your uncle.'

They moved into the tackroom and Mark struck a match to light the lamp on the desk next to the door. There were two stout chairs next to it. In the back corner of the room, there was a camp-bed along the wall. It was covered with a bright-colored Indian blanket and had another one folded at the foot of it. Near the center of the room was a small potbellied stove which crackled pleasantly with a glowing fire inside, and a blackened coffee pot on top of it.

Mark settled himself behind the desk and Clint took the chair at the side, facing the old man. Then, lighting up one of his few remaining cigars, Clint relaxed.

'I'm the one who wrote you that letter,' Mark informed him, and seeing the puzzled expression on Clint's face, he explained. 'There's no reason to be surprised, Clint. Old Jeff can't even sign his own name, much less write letters.'

Mark chuckled fondly, and said: 'Top of that, the stubborn old cuss would of let 'em burn him out 'fore he'd ask for help. No sir, I don't believe old Jeff would ask for a bucket of water if'n his clothes was on fire.'

'Then how did you know to write me?' Clint asked. He could tell that Tollett and Uncle Jeff were the best of friends by the few words that had been said.

'Wasn't hard. Jeff mentioned your name once or twice, and I associated you at once. Bein' in this business, I've heard 'bout you, so I wrote to that outfit you was workin' for down in New Mexico Territory when you was ridin' shotgun out of Fort Summer.'

He scratched his gray stubble, and

continued. 'Yep, when all this claim jumpin' started, I happened to remember and wrote you there hopin' someone would know where you was, and send the letter on to you.'

'I got the letter two weeks ago,' Clint informed him.

'Of course, I didn't rightly know what to expect when I wrote you like that, but I kind of figured if'n you were half the man old Jeff was in his day, then you'd work out. You've already got a bit of a reputation on yourself.'

'I didn't know that,' Clint said.

'Yep, sure do. Now when you see old Jeff, it just might be a good idea if'n you told him you just happened to be in this neck of the woods. Jeff might not take kindly to the idea of us wet-nursin' him. Kind of set in his ways old Jeff is,' Mark said, then chuckled. He took another minute to build up a stream of juice, which went accurately into a spittoon next to the desk.

During the lull in the talk, the kids came into the tackroom, and Tollett waved them toward the bed, and said: 'Sit over there, and if'n you feel sleepy, go 'head and stretch out. You've both had a night.'

57

Kevin walked over to the bed and sat down, but Mary busied herself by pouring coffee, which she brought over to the desk. When she handed Clint his cup, she looked at him with more than a mild interest, which Tollett was quick to perceive. At Clint's, 'Thanks, Mary,' she blushed slightly and quickly turned away, which caused him to look at her in surprise.

Then Mary walked over to the bed, sat down next to Kevin, and watched intently as the two men drank the hot coffee. She couldn't understand what it was about Clint that held her attention, but she did know from the first moment he challenged the bully, Bert Turner, at Joe's place that evening, that Clint couldn't have been more handsome and chivalrous than if he'd been wearing shining armor like the knights in the books she sometimes read.

Mary felt a strange sensation inside when she regarded him, and his touch when she'd nested in his coat had both thrilled and comforted her. She now thought she knew how a young bird feels in its mother's nest: safe, protected, and warm.

As she studied his unkempt appearance, Mary saw past the rough range clothes, unshaven face, and untrimmed hair to the man beneath. She could see that Clint was both gentle and good, but at the same time, he was ruthless and cold when defending the rights of the weak and helpless; exactly like a knight in the days of old. Just being in his presence gave her a warm, melting glow of contentment.

Tollett looked at Clint with a grin and with a chuckle, and said: 'Clint, you sure didn't waste any time steppin' on the right toes in Pine Creek. Them two you tangled with at Joe's works for Silk Barrister, and Joe is in cahoots with Silk in some way. Of course, I wouldn't say that in public, and if'n I was you, I'd watch my backtrail real careful from here out.'

Taking a sip of the hot coffee, Clint could feel the girl's green eyes watching his every move, and it made him wonder if something was unbuttoned for him to be receiving so much attention from her.

Glancing at Tollett, Clint said: 'What were their names? We didn't get into any formalities at the time.'

'The big one is Bert Turner, the town bully. The short one is Kelly Webber. He's called Nails, 'cause that's what he loads his big, double-barreled Greener with. Nails is the one to watch out for. You should've killed him when you had the chance, 'cause he's a dry-gulcher if'n I ever saw one, and if'n he recoveres, he'll be lookin' for you.'

'I don't think he'll make it,' Clint said evenly. 'Besides, I always keep a good lookout behind me. An Injun might get to me, but never a white man.'

'Too bad everyone ain't like that,' Mark said quietly.

'How's that?'

'Durin' the past few months, there's been three miners turned up missin'. One of 'em was found the other day with his back full of horseshoe nails. Right after each one disappeared, Silk Barrister showed up with papers to their claims, sayin' those miners had sold to him 'fore they left town; said they'd planned to pull out and go home. At least that's what Silk told folks around town. The men know what's goin' on, but they don't figure it's healthy to ask questions, and everyone watches their backtrails as best they can,' Mark said, then spit again, hitting the spittoon with a dull plunk.

Clint relit the stogie and thought over what Mark had told him. It was the usual story of robbery and murder, along with claim jumping, and all that one normally heard about any new gold field. He puffed on the stogie for a minute and asked,

'Mark, just where does Uncle Jeff fit into all this?'

'Well, back 'bout three months ago, Jeff got another assay done on his mine, and it came up highgrade, or near to it. And it's lookin' better all the time. Right after that is when Silk Barrister and his crowd began to try to freeze him out by not sellin' him supplies, and even takin' pot-shots at him when he stuck his head outta the mine. It's real puzzlin' too, 'cause Jeff didn't tell no one except me 'bout it. The assayer knows of course. His name's Dan Perkins, but I ain't been able to learn nothin' 'bout him.'

'How come the miners ain't formed a committee to put Barrister and his gang of skunks outta business?' Clint asked. 'It appears to me that it's past time to take care of him.'

'Because the men are all scared, that's why,' Mark replied bitterly. 'Silk and his gunnies have everybody runnin' down-wind, and they're too scared to spit for fear it'll blow back in their faces. Silk's got four real tough gunnies workin' for him now; Cole Neyland, Tom and Pete Clayton, and a half-breed Apache named Chu'ta. All the rest of his crowd are just saloon toughs without much backbone, except when they got the edge on a man.'

Clint knew of the four gunfighters that Tollett had named by their reputations. He had a nodding acquaintance with Cole Neyland, who was said to be one of the fastest men in the west with a six gun. Clint had seen Chu'ta one time in Tucson, and heard talk that he was a mean one to tangle with. The Clayton brothers he knew only by their reputations; they were fast, but they liked to get an edge on a man and usually tried to 'box' their intended victims. With that kind of opposition, it was no wonder the miners were afraid. Those four gunfighters had probably killed half a hundred men between them.

'It surely does sound like a problem all right,' Clint said quietly. 'I've heard of all those boys, but the only one I've seen in action is Cole Neyland. He killed Billy Lee Parker in Carson City 'bout a year ago, and Billy Lee was hell on wheels with a six-shooter.'

'Yeah,' Mark said, 'and what's worse, Silk's havin' a mite of trouble smokin' old Jeff out, and his reputation's startin' to suffer. He made his brags and now everyone's waitin' to see if he can pull it off.

'Old Jeff's holed up in the Sweet Lady with that old Sharps rifle of his,' Mark continued, 'and said he'll shoot anybody that sets foot on his claim. He will, too. Since everybody knows it, everyone walks a wide path around the Sweet Lady. So far, Silk Barrister ain't been able to find anyone to go up there and persuade old Jeff to either sell out, or else get out. Silk won't neither as long as Jeff stays holed up with that big Sharps of his,' Mark said, his pride in Jeff apparent in his voice and eyes, which sparkled with mischievous lights.

'If'n he's holed up in the mine, and has been for so long, then how come Silk hasn't been able to starve him out?' Clint asked.

Tollett chuckled good naturedly, then spit a long stream of tobacco juice as he looked at Clint craftily.

'Old Silk and his crew been wonderin' the same thin' themselves these past two months,' Mark said, chuckling again. 'Old Jeff's been gettin' his groceries and water by special messenger—a timber wolf!'

Surprise registered on Clint's face, and both the kids sat up straighter to catch every word about the wolf and the man who could tame one.

'Got you wonderin', huh?' Mark laughed, then continued with merriment in his amber eyes. 'Well, that's how it's done. A few years ago Old Jeff found a wolf's den and the bitch attacked him. He had to kill her. Then he found out that she had a litter. So, bein' a lonesome kind'a man, he took one of the pups for company and raised him like a dog. Twice a week, that gray wolf sneaks down here with saddle bags strapped to his back, and I fill 'em up. Then he sneaks back to the mine.'

Tollett paused to take another spit, then continued. 'Silk keeps Jeff's claim staked out in shifts, but they still ain't figured out what's happenin'. That's a right smart wolf too, and meaner than a den of rattlesnakes. He won't let nobody touch him but Jeff, and barely tolerates me puttin' that grub in 'em bags. He just stands there and growls the whole time. Yep, it sure does give me the shivers bein' close to him. It's like baitin' a real touchy bear trap that's already been set.'

Clint had to smile at the reference to bear traps, having had considerable experience with them down Texas when those ranchers had wanted to invite him to a party.

'Mark, it don't sound to me like either one of you are lackin' any screws,' Clint said with admiration. 'From the sound of it, you two are more'n a match for the likes of Silk Barrister and his bunch so far.'

Tollett's eyes went serious and he said gravely: 'Yeah, we've been holdin' our own, but the trouble is, old Jeff will have to come out sometime or another, or they'll blast him out if'n they don't seal him up in the mine. If'n he does come out, they'll gun him down in the street without a by-your-leave.'

Clint knew there wasn't any doubt about that. Cole Neyland was a gunfighter who usually hired his gun out on a straight commission basis, and was as cold-blooded a killer as could be found west of the Mississippi River. He was a slow talker, soft spoken, and well educated man with a good family background. Cole was always meticulously groomed, even something of a dandy, and visited the barber shop at least once a day when he could. Rumor had it that Cole had once been a school master and came from a well-to-do family back east. But Cole Neyland had no compunctions about shooting a man face to face, or even in the back. He always finished a job he was hired to do, no matter how he did it.

Also, he was fast with a gun; real fast. But even more, he was a dead shot; always shooting for the head 'or heart, and Cole had never been known to miss. There were many men who were faster than Cole: Bat Masterson, Wyatt Earp, Doc Holiday, and the likes. The only one who might have held his own in accuracy with him was Wild Bill Hickok. The other men might miss, but not Cole Neyland or Wild Bill.

Neyland had twenty graves to his credit. He probably had a lot more that people didn't know about, except the person who paid him for his deadly talent. Cole wasn't a man who went around bragging about his kills, so there was no way of knowing for sure.

Chu'ta was different in a lot of ways from Cole Neyland, but just as deadly; if not more so. Being a half-breed Apache, he'd spent most of his boyhood years in Cochise's band; and Cochise was as wily a fighter as had ever eluded the U.S. Cavalry. However, Chu'ta got caught by the cavalry and the whim of a young second lieutenant spared his life.

The Army turned Chu'ta over to a

Catholic mission and they taught him the ways of the white man; knowledge that he used now in his chosen profession, which he enjoyed tremendously and worked at with relish.

Chu'ta discovered that there was no need to kill whites for nothing, as other whites would pay good gold dollars for that, and he needed the gold to buy his whisky and tobacco. He thought it was a good joke to get paid for doing what he would have done for nothing.

He was something of a puzzle, because outside of being known as a hired killer, nothing else was known about him. He rarely spoke or let any emotions show on his face. He was loyal to his employer as long as it suited him, and once wronged in any way, he would turn like a viper and strike at both ends. Silk Barrister was well advised to be very careful in his treatment to the redskin, or Silk just might learn he had let a snake into the henhouse.

Clint thought over everything that Mark had told him and what he already knew. Then he glanced over at the bed and saw that both youngsters had fallen asleep while he and Mark were talking. Catching Mark's eyes, he motioned toward the door of the tackroom. Then both men got up and eased quietly out of the room.

Outside the room, Clint leaned against a stall and asked: 'Mark, how can I get to the Sweet Lady?'

'Clint, I sure wouldn't advise you to go up there at night. Old Jeff might put a bullet in you by mistake, and he'd feel downright bad 'bout it when he found out who you are,' Mark said seriously.

'Don't worry none 'bout it, just tell me how to get there. If'n things are as bad as you say, then what we need right now is some fast action 'fore everythin' blows up in our faces, and they find out who I am and why I've come. It won't take long either once things get to poppin' around here.'

From the dim glow of the lantern, Tollett could see the stubborn lines in Clint's face, and knew it would be useless to argue with him, so he gave in immediately.

'Okay Clint, if'n you're dead set on stoppin' a bullet, don't let it be said I never tried to talk you outta it. The mine is located about half a mile northeast of here. It's right beside the Fancy Nance, and it has a big sign on it with warnin' posters just as plain as day. You'd better leave your horse here, or both of you'll end up at the bottom of a deserted mine shaft.'

'All right, Mark.'

'Don't fret 'bout him. I'll give him a good feed and look out for him,' Mark said, then proceeded to give accurate directions on how to reach the mine, including how best to avoid the man Silk Barrister had hired to watch the place.

'Mark, I don't want to avoid him,' Clint said. 'I think I'll have a little talk with the jasper and see if'n I can't make a Christian outta him. Kind'a teach him the error of his ways, so to speak.'

'Heh, heh,' Mark chuckled, and said: 'Ding-blastit, if'n you ain't the spittin' image of your Uncle Jeff. Yes sirree, smartest thin' I ever done was writin' that letter to you. But, you don't say nothin' to old Jeff 'bout it; you hear, boy?'

'I won't, Mark. I value my own hide too much to get the old man mad at me. Besides, I know those Pickens are hell to tangle with when they get wound up,' Clint said.

After Tollett finished giving him directions, he reached into his saddle bags and pulled out a pair of moccasin boots a

69

Navajo girl had made for him a long time ago. They were still in good shape and had been resoled several times over the years. The tops were beaded and soft as a baby's skin. Clint pulled them on after removing his stiff, high-heeled boots.

Kneeling down, he pulled the rawhide laces tight and tied them, then stood up and removed another item from the saddle bags. It was a long Spanish knife with a thin, evil-looking blade of blue steel. When Clint slipped it into the top of the moccasins, Tollett gave a low whistle at the sight of the blade.

'Clint, that's quite a pig sticker you've got there. Mighty wicked looking; it sure is. How'd you happen to come by a knife like it?' Mark asked curiously.

'I won it off a Spanish don down in Sonora one night, and dang near broke his heart when I wouldn't sell it back to him the next mornin',' Clint replied, then moved toward the open door of the stable with Mark following.

Pausing by the doorway, Clint turned to Tollett and said quietly: 'Mark, I don't know how all this is gonna turn out, so if'n anythin' happens to me, I'd like you to sell my horse and gear, then give all the money to those kids in there. Then see to it that they get some kind of a start away from here. Mind doin' that for me?'

'Sure, sure. Don't worry none 'bout them youngsters,' Mark assured him gruffly. 'You be careful, hear! Don't go steppin' in no bear traps.'

'Those things were made for bears,' Clint replied, 'and I don't reckon I fit the description yet, even with all my hair and beard.'

With those words, Clint slipped out the door, and was instantly swallowed up by the darkness. After a minute, Tollett peered outside, but saw nothing of Clint. With a dry chuckle, he turned and retraced his steps to the tackroom.

Tollett felt sure that things were going to start boiling pretty quickly. That young nephew of old Jeff's was going to liven things up around Pine Creek, and Tollett chuckled to himself in anticipation of the excitement.

Entering the tackroom, he crossed to the camp-bed and spread a blanket over the two youngsters. The girl was young, but Tollett knew that inside she burned with the fires of young womanhood. He hadn't missed the shining looks she'd given Clint, him smelling like a hog and looking like the wildest mountain man that ever came down outta the hills. Tollett knew that was the way of it. Women weren't rational creatures anyhow, and besides, she could do a lot worse than someone like Clint Jackson. He might not live to an old age, but he'd give her the best that was in him.

Thinking about young love, and the coming excitement, it was with a happy heart that he blew out the lamp on the desk and felt his way outside to the hay stack. Tollett spread a couple of blankets on the stack of hay and pulled off his boots, then lay down to get himself some sleep, if he could.

CHAPTER FOUR

Outside the stable, Clint paused for a moment to let his eyes adjust to the darkness. Then he moved slowly northward along the side of the muddy road.

While he'd been inside the stable talking, the wind had died down to a whisper and the rain had quit altogether. The dark sky now held only scattered clouds that drifted slowly southward, and as they passed, they let the moonlight break through with a soft, silvery glow.

The tents and buildings of Pine Creek fell behind, and Clint could feel the wet ground beneath his moccasined feet. It was soft, but since it hadn't been used by wagons and horses since the rain, it wasn't churned into mud like the town street had been.

At least something was on his side right from the start. The soft ground would muffle any small sounds he might make in the moccasins, and enable him to move very quietly.

After listening to Tollett's story, Clint concluded that action had to be taken quickly, and for that, he had the element of surprise on his side. Nobody outside of Tollett and the two kids knew who he was, or what he'd come to Pine Creek for. Clint knew that if he could strike a hard blow at the opposition before Silk Barrister found out about him, then they just might get nervous and make a mistake. The least that could happen was they'd get a scare thrown into them when an unknown element entered the game.

So far, Silk Barrister and his bunch hadn't had any active opposition, so they were probably off guard, relaxed and careless. If Clint had any say in the matter, Silk Barrister was going to find out that messing around with the Jackson-Pickens clan was a very unhealthy occupation.

They weren't going to like the way he fought, either, because Jacksons fought dirty when they had to; hitting their enemies where it would hurt them the worst, regardless of the consequences. But then, Silk Barrister and his bunch of skunks didn't deserve to walk on the same ground with decent folks, and it set Clint's blood to boiling just thinking about what they had gotten away with so far.

Silk Barrister thought that he was the only rooster in the henhouse, but the way Clint figured things, what Silk needed was for somebody to pluck a few of his tail feathers. That might cramp his style of strutting, and Clint thought he was just the man to handle the job.

While he was doing all that speculating, he managed to get close to Uncle Jeff's mine. Stopping for a moment in the dark cover of a large boulder, Clint decided it would be a good idea to get the lay of things

74

before stomping in. He knew he needed to learn the ground he might be fighting over.

Moving carefully around the boulder, he squatted down on his heels to take in his surroundings. Although the wind had died down, it was getting colder, so he flexed his fingers to keep the blood circulating. The last thing he needed was to have stiff hands when his life might depend upon his being able to use them quickly.

Tollett had said that Silk Barrister was keeping Uncle Jeff's mine staked out in shifts from near the Fancy Nance mine. Clint figured he'd better find the stakeout man so there wouldn't be any worrying about getting shot in the back. It might be hard enough getting inside the mine shack without being shot by Uncle Jeff, much less having to worry about one of Barrister's hired skunks knocking him off.

Clint had a little bit of experience in the art of manhunting. From time to time, he'd done some scouting for the Army, since they had dumb fool notions of keeping the Apaches penned up in one place. There are some things that a man learns pretty fast when he's chasing Apaches: he won't ever catch an Apache unless the Indian wants to be caught, and he'll never see one until the

Apache wants to be seen. But, right now, it wasn't Apaches he was after. He was looking for a cold and hungry white man who was doing guard duty on a barren hillside. That alone changed things considerably, and made Clint's work somewhat easier.

After a while, if a man lives long enough, some of the Apache ways rub off on him, and start to affect how he does things. Contrary to popular belief, in many ways an Indian is a better fighting man than a white man. And of all the Indian warriors, the Apache is the best.

Squatting in the cover of the boulder and searching the darkness with his eyes, Clint spotted the entrance to the Fancy Nance mine. It was to his right and about fifty yards away. Then, using it to get his bearings, he found the dark shape of what had to be the Sweet Lady mine shack where Tollett said Uncle Jeff was holed up.

The shack was to the left and about sixty yards off. Even with the occasional breaks in the clouds, which let through the soft glow of moonlight, Clint was unable to see any sign of life in or around the shack. But years ago, he'd learned the hard way that looks can be deceiving, and he still carried the scar from an Apache knife to remember the lesson by. The problem he had now was getting a rope on the polecat that Silk Barrister had sitting in the dark somewhere.

Now that he had his bearings, Clint found what Tollett had told him to look for. Between the Fancy Nance and the Sweet Lady, the ground was fairly smooth and sloped upward to the Fancy Nance, so the dark pile that Clint saw had to be timber supports. They stood out in the occasional moonlight like a beaver's dam, and that was where Clint expected to find the stake-out man.

Crouching low, he eased toward the pile of timbers as he moved to the side and below it, being careful not to move too fast, or make any noise which might tip off the guard. The soft, damp ground helped to muffle the small noises he made, but he moved slowly. Motion has a way of catching a man's eye; even in the dark. Clint wanted his surprise to remain unspoiled.

On reaching the pile of timbers, he straightened up slowly and leaned against the pile gently, then gripped the worn butt of the Remington and eased it out of the holster. At the same instant, a match flared not three or four feet away from where he stood. It was on the other side of the pile and just around the corner. Then came a muttered curse as the match fizzed out, and a second later another match flared briefly. Clint could smell the smoke of a cigarette being lit, so he made his move, quickly and silently.

Clint hadn't expected things would be this easy for him, even though he knew things hardly ever work out according to plan. At least this time, he wasn't getting the short end of the stick.

The stake-out man had done plenty by lighting the cigarette. It not only told Clint exactly where he was, but, also, when a man lights a cigarette at night, or looks into a camp fire, he will be night-blinded for a few seconds after he puts out the match, or looks away from the fire. That was what Clint was counting on at that very moment.

Moving swiftly, he stepped around the corner of the timber pile and saw the guard standing with his back to him, leaning against the timbers smoking the cigarette and watching the mine shack below. The guard, completely oblivious to his immediate surroundings, was but two feet away from Clint. The man probably didn't like the idea of having to stand out in the cold night by himself watching the old man's mine shack, and Clint figured to make him like it even less.

Quietly stepping up behind the man, Clint stuck the cold barrel of the forty-four revolver behind the man's ear, and cocked the hammer; those four clicks spelling death with a voice that left no room for speculation.

The man stiffened as if he'd been struck by a bolt of lightning. Then before he fully realized what was happening, Clint pulled the guard's gun from his holster to make him a little more reasonable. When the man started to turn around, Clint nudged him none too gently with the gun barrel, and spoke softly into his ear.

'Mister, if'n you want to keep your ear and half of your head along with it, then it just might be a real good idea if'n you didn't get this gun of mine upset by movin' around too much. It would be right shameful if'n it sent off because you made it nervous.'

The man read the message clearly and held himself very still. He didn't know who was behind him, or what manner of a man

Clint was. He knew that whoever was behind him was a sneaky fellow, and that was reason enough to be cautious. The guard didn't even move when Clint reached down and shoved the barrel of the gun into the soft ground, filling it with mud up to the cylinder, and then dropped it back into his holster.

'L-look m-mister,' the man stuttered nervously.

'Shut up!' Clint snapped coldly, then pulled the Spanish knife from the top of his moccasin. 'I don't want to hear anythin' you've got to say.'

Sliding the thin, razor-sharp blade under the man's gunbelt and pant's belt, Clint pulled the blade upward and felt the leather part as the steel cut easily through. The man felt his pants and gun starting to fall, and quickly grabbed them.

'I think you're startin' to get the idea,' Clint said quietly. 'Now, while you're busy holdin' up your pants, I want you to listen real close to what I'm goin' to tell you.'

'Y-yes s-sir,' he stuttered.

'Personally, I don't think Silk Barrister is payin' you enough to die, mister, and that's exactly what's goin' to happen to you if'n I ever see your face in Pine Creek after tonight. You'll just get one chance to get out with your hide, and this is it. Besides, I know you, and you don't know me. Next time we meet, I won't use this knife to give you somethin' to do, because you're goin' to meet your ancestors, and you won't be comin' back from the meetin'. Now, do you follow what I'm tellin' you?'

'Y-yes s-sir,' he replied.

'I'm right glad to hear that,' Clint said evenly. 'When I turn you loose, I'd use them paws of yours to hold up your britches if'n I was you. It just might be a good idea if'n you were to clean that gun of yours 'fore you tried to shoot anythin'. It just might blow up in your face, it bein' full of mud like it is. You still listenin'?' Clint asked, nudging him with the barrel of the forty-four.

'Y-yeah, I'm listening,' he answered quickly.

'Good! I've got some more advice for you. Did you ever hear the story in the Good Book 'bout Lot's wife? How the Good Lord told her not to look back when they left the city?'

'Y-yeah, I've heard it, mister,' he replied.

'Well, mister, you'd better take it to

heart, 'cause I won't turn you into no pillar of salt. I ain't near as fancy as the Lord 'bout them things, but I get the job done. You get the drift?'

'Y-yes s-sir,' he answered, worried.

'That's mighty fine. I hope you've got more sense than Nails had; poor jasper, I wasn't even tryin' to kill him, either. You're gettin' a chance to get out; Nails is stayin', sort of permanent like.'

'Nails?' the man asked questioningly.

'Gone, poor fellow, or near to it. Last I saw, he was tryin' to cough lead outta his lungs, and that ain't a good sign. And Bert Turner wasn't lookin' none too healthy either. Sure would hate to have to do the same for you,' Clint said, his voice tinged with regret.

'You won't, mister,' the man said earnestly, knowing that if the stranger had gotten Nails and Bert, he had to be a rough character. 'I'm clearing out tonight.'

'All right then, get goin'!' Clint ordered and gave him a shove to start him on his way.

The man half stumbled and half ran down the hill, then disappeared into the darkness on his way toward town. Once Clint was sure that the man was gone and not likely to return, he holstered the forty-four and slipped the knife back into its nesting place in the top of his moccasin.

He knew it might have been foolish to let the stake-out man go, but he believed a man was entitled to one mistake; the same as a dog is entitled to one bite. The man had made his mistake when he hired out to Silk Barrister, but now he had a chance to set that straight. Clint didn't hold with killing unless there was no way to get around it, and he hoped that the little talk he and the man had had would soak in. But if it didn't, then Clint would keep his word and kill the jasper on sight; after giving him a fair chance to draw.

Now the problem Clint faced was how to get close enough to the mine shack to talk with Uncle Jeff without getting perforated by a Sharps rifle. There was no way of knowing when the old man slept, or if he was asleep now. To wake him suddenly before he found out who was outside just might cause him to commence shooting.

Then there was the wolf. The animal was sure to be listening for any sounds outside the shack, and would either wake the old man, or attack. Now that was worth considering because a wolf is about twice as mean and three times stronger than a dog and quite capable of ripping a man to shreds.

There was no way that Uncle Jeff would be expecting anybody outside of the shack except Silk Barrister's gunnies, so he was most likely a mite trigger happy. If he was, it wouldn't be good for Clint's health, since the Pickens were as accurate with guns as the Jacksons were.

After deliberating on the problem for a while, Clint decided that there was just one way to do it. The only thing that could possibly go wrong would be for Uncle Jeff to fill him full of holes. The thought that he was family didn't make the fact go down any easier. Still, there wasn't much choice about it.

With his mind made up, Clint pulled a cigar out of his shirt pocket and struck a match. Once the cigar was going good, he stepped away from the timber pile in full view of the Sweet Lady mine shack, and knew that Uncle Jeff probably had the big Sharps rifle, hammer laid back, aimed at him at that very moment. It was enough to give a man goose bumps. Then Clint broke into a song in a loud voice as he began to walk toward the shack.

The song was 'Sam Drew's Mule,' and was once popular back in the North Carolina mountains, and even down in Texas. It was an old song and not one that was heard often any more. As he walked, Clint held his hands out from his body, and hoped that Uncle Jeff's eyesight was still all right. It was mighty dark, even with the glow from the moon, and Clint wasn't silhouetted, since he had the rising of the hill directly behind him.

Clint's singing voice had never been very good, and the best he could hope for was that Uncle Jeff would at least be able to recognize the tune. He was taking a pretty thin chance, but he just couldn't think of anything else to try. With each step he made toward the shack, the more Clint began to doubt his own sanity.

When he was about thirty feet from the shack he was ready to give up the whole idea when a raspy old voice put a stop to his off-tune singing.

'Mister, you can just stop right there, and quit that dad-blame hollerin' a'fore you run off the whole dang countryside!' came a yell from inside the shack. 'Now either you're plum dang crazy, an infernal jackass fool, or else just plain darn stupid. I'm

85

mighty curious to find out which one you are a'fore I blow a big hole in ya, so you better start jawin', and it'd better be gospel, mister!' Uncle Jeff warned seriously.

'Uncle Jeff,' Clint called out loudly, 'don't you start gettin' itchy fingered with that old Sharps. It's Clint Jackson out here, and ma sure wouldn't take it kindly if'n her brother was to shoot one of her boys.'

'Mister, who're you unclin' 'round here?' Uncle Jeff demanded querulously. 'How'd I know you ain't one of 'em darn polecats who's tryin' to steal my gold mine?'

'You don't, Uncle Jeff, 'til you stop your jabberin' and ask me some questions that only a Jackson can answer,' Clint replied.

'Don't you start smart mouthin' me, you youn' squirt, 'cause you ain't no kin of mine 'till I say you are,' he said sharply, then asked: 'Now, what's your ma's name?'

'It's Pickens, same as yours is. Elizabeth Marie Pickens, and she's your sister,' Clint replied, then began to move toward the shack.

'Mister, you take one more step, and you're a dead man,' Uncle Jeff warned. 'I ain't decided 'bout you yet. You may be a Jackson, and then, you might not be. I ain't takin' no chances; you hear!'

'Yep, I hear you Uncle Jeff,' Clint answered with impatience in his voice. 'You're askin' the questions, or are you goin' to keep me standin' out here all dan' night while you make up your mind if'n I'm kinfolks or not?'

'You're sure sassy 'nuff to be a Jackson,' Uncle Jeff admitted. 'Just tell me where you learned that tune you was makin' suffer so blame much.'

'I'll tell you more'n that Uncle Jeff,' Clint replied. 'Then I'm through with you. Ma said you used to sing that song all the time when you two were kids. She also told me that you have a scar on your backside where she laid a hot poker to you for pickin' on her once.'

'Heh, heh,' Uncle Jeff chuckled from inside the shack. 'Yep, she sure did it all right.' Then he asked raspingly: 'How's your ma doin' boy?'

'I ain't been home in so lon', that I ain't got no idea,' Clint answered. 'But the last I heard, she was just fine.'

'Well, boy, don't just stand out there jawin' like a dan' mule. Come on in and pick yourself a corner,' Uncle Jeff said, chuckling.

87

CHAPTER FIVE

Walking toward the mine shack, Clint took in the details of its construction. His uncle had built it big, and to last.

The walls were of granite rock, which had been blasted out of the mine, and the roof was flat with mining timbers laid side by side, with a layer of rock over it and a foot of sod over the rocks. The whole building was square-shaped, about thirty feet by thirty feet. It was big for a mining shack, more like a house, but a fort might be a better description because there weren't any windows; just rifle slits built into the walls.

It was easy to see why Silk Barrister and his bunch of gunnies were having so much trouble getting Uncle Jeff out. It would take an army, complete with artillery, to blast him out of a position like that, and Clint didn't envy the chore Barrister had taken on for himself.

But something puzzled Clint. He couldn't see the mine shaft anywhere, or anything which resembled an opening to a mine tunnel on the steep slant on the hillside. He knew the mine had to be close by for Uncle Jeff to be holed up in the shack guarding it.

When he reached the solid-looking door, Clint waited in front of it and listened to his uncle remove the cross-bars which held the door shut. After a minute, the door opened and Clint slipped inside and heard the cross-bars being replaced. Then he heard another sound within the inky blackness of the room.

At first it sounded like the deep, distant rumble of cannon fire, or a coming thunderstorm, but not exactly. It was too close. Clint couldn't see a thing, but suddenly he knew what was causing the rumbling sound.

It was the deepest, meanest, and most ominous growl that he'd ever heard, and it came from somewhere off to his left, and seemed to be moving closer with each passing second. It was the timber wolf that Mark Tollett had told him about, and the information had slipped his mind when he was talking to Uncle Jeff.

Clint knew now why Tollett felt jittery just being around the wolf. He felt the same way and the hair on his neck started to rise. He expected to feel those teeth sink into him at any moment.

'Boy, just stay right still and don't make any sudden moves, and you'll be all right,' Uncle Jeff said, then speaking more harshly, he spoke to the wolf: 'Moses, quieten down!'

But Moses didn't quieten down as he'd been told, and the deep growl continued without interruption while Uncle Jeff moved to the center of the room and fumbled with a lantern. A few seconds later, he struck a match and as the wick caught on the lantern, Clint saw what was making the rumbling growl. The sight was even worse than the sound.

Standing stiff-legged with its hackles raised and sharp teeth bared was the largest slate gray timber wolf that Clint had ever seen. He was about four feet away and slightly to the left. The wolf's yellow-green eyes were locked on Clint's gray ones with a fierce anticipation, and he was tensed, ready to spring into instant action at a single word from his master. It wasn't a good feeling to know that you were the sole object of the wolf's attention.

'Moses! Quit now, he's friendly. Quit!' Uncle Jeff ordered firmly.

The growling stopped, then, with a kind

of snort, Moses turned and gave Clint
another distrustful look as he walked stiff-
legged over to Uncle Jeff and sat down
beside him; his mouth open and his tongue
hanging out, just like a dog. But the effect
was lost with the unblinking stare which he
regarded Clint with, and the message was
very clear. The wolf seemed to be saying:
'You got away from me this time, but
there's always the future to consider!' A
man could tell the wolf thought the odds
were on his side, and Clint hated to admit it
to himself, but the wolf was probably right.

'Boy, come on over and sit a spell. Old
Moses here is just bein' particular. He's
like that, kind'a distrustful, Moses is,' he
said, his voice affectionate as he laid a hand
on the wolf's large head.

With the wolf acting fairly docile, Clint
was finally able to take a minute to study
his uncle, who he'd never seen before.
From all the rip-roaring tales that were told
about Jeff Pickens, he'd expected to see a
giant of a man. But Uncle Jeff wasn't a
giant; in fact, he looked kind of average.

The old man stood about five-feet, ten-
inches tall, and weighed around a hundred
and forty pounds, but he looked to be
solidly built for a man in his sixties. He

wore no shirt, but the suspenders holding up his mud-brown, baggy pants, which were tucked into flat-heeled boots, rested on red, woolen, winter longhandles, which were buttoned down the front with small white buttons.

A long mane of thick white hair, which looked as though it hadn't seen a pair of clippers in a long time, hung to the neck of the longhandles. What arrested Clint's attention were the piercing gray eyes, which were like his own. They were like two cool pools of alertness in the dark, deeply seamed face, and appeared to be able to look right through a man.

Uncle Jeff's nose was prominent, beaklike, jutting out from his face, and was carried proudly. It was a distinctive type of nose. The rest of his face was lost in the grayness of his sweeping mustache and beard, which hid his lips, chin, and jaw from view.

'What're you starin' at, boy?' Uncle Jeff demanded. 'Ain't you ever seen an old coot a'fore?' His voice was playful, not querulous as it had been earlier. 'Come and sit, boy, you make me nervous by towerin' over me like that.'

Clint walked over to the rough-hewed

table and lowered himself into a stout homemade chair, giving another glance at the timber wolf. From the spiteful look the wolf gave him, Clint saw that he hadn't changed his attitude one bit.

'How come you named him Moses?' Clint asked. 'He don't look none too holy to me, unless it'd be a holy terror.'

The gray beard moved into what appeared to be a grin as Uncle Jeff chuckled softly. 'Yep, he does have that look 'bout him, don't he?' Uncle Jeff agreed. 'Well, him and the gent in the Good Book had one thin' in common, and that's separatin' things.'

'How's that, Uncle Jeff?'

'Well now, the gent in the Book was good at separatin' the Red Sea, but old Moses here, he's good at doin' the same thin' with people. Why he can walk into a crowd of folks, and they'll open up just like he was one of 'em ferrin' kings or somethin'.'

'Yep, I can see your point,' Clint replied.

They fell silent for a few moments. Jeff began to load a clay pipe with coarse-cut tobacco, and Clint relit his cigar that had gone out. After lighting up, both men leaned back, the smoke hanging like blue clouds around them.

Uncle Jeff never appeared to look directly at him for long at a time, but Clint knew he was being critically examined at every second. Finally, Uncle Jeff broke the silence.

'Yep, you're a Jackson all right. You got your eyes, but you got the Jackson build and height. Heh, heh,' he chuckled, then said: 'You missed the Pickens' nose, though; lucky for you.'

Clint smiled at the comment, not seeing anything wrong with the Pickens' nose, as Uncle Jeff called it. It was kind of proud-looking and determined, with character, Clint thought, like an Indian, and he admired a lot of Indians.

'I'm kind'a puzzled though,' Uncle Jeff continued. 'What're you doin' here? Last I hears, you was down in New Mexico. What brings you so far north, boy?'

'Well Uncle Jeff, I got kind'a tired of ridin' shot-gun, then I got tired of sittin' in line shacks. I figured there had to be somethin' better a man could do for a livin' than watchin' other folks' money and cattle. Since I had a pretty good grub-stake in my poke, I decided to try my hand at a little prospectin',' Clint explained. 'Then I remembered hearin' you was somewhere around Pine Creek, so I decided to drop by and say howdy, and maybe have a drink or two with you. But it seems that folks 'round here ain't very sociable to strangers.'

Clint proceeded to tell Uncle Jeff everything that had happened since he'd gotten into town including all that Mark Tollett had told him, but he left out the part about Tollett writing the letter.

As far as Clint could tell, Uncle Jeff swallowed the tale, hook, line and sinker, as he sat back and gave it some thought.

'It ain't your fight, boy,' he said finally. 'Your ma wouldn't take too kindly to me gettin' you mixed up in this ruckus, and I sure don't want your ma riled up at me. Old Silk Barrister and his bunch of polecats ain't nothin' compared to your ma when she gets in a temper. I've got personal experience when it comes to Elizabeth's temper.' His beard moved again into a grin as he gave a chuckle.

'Uncle Jeff, I'm not goin' to sit here and contradict my elders. Ma raised me better'n that, and you know how ma sets store by such things. But, the way I see it, I don't rightly see how ma even comes into this at all. In fact, the way I look at things, Silk Barrister is responsible for what's happenin' in Pine Creek by importin' gunfighters and bullies, and lettin' kids get pushed 'round, and all that. Now Barrister's got himself on my bad side. Besides, some low-down skunk done stole my slicker. This just ain't a law 'bidin' place, and needs to be straightened up a mite.'

'Well, boy . . .'

'I just figured that seein' as how you and Barrister ain't exactly friendly, you might want to join the party and have some fun outta him a'fore I ruin his little game. I would sure hate for you to say I was greedy and didn't give you a chance to help out your kinfolks.'

'Well . . .' Uncle Jeff tried to speak again.

'Besides, bein' a Jackson and a Pickens, it just wouldn't do to turn tail and run. Nope, it just wouldn't look good for the family name if'n I did that, and I sure wouldn't be able to look ma in the eyes again. Family sticks together, Uncle Jeff.' Clint finished on that note and sat back, waiting to see if his uncle swallowed it all.

Uncle Jeff's eyes had narrowed as he

listened to Clint, and he gave him sharp looks throughout the whole conversation as he puffed on his clay pipe. Finally he snorted, and said: 'I've seen some long-winded fools in my time, but you 'bout top the cake. I got the feelin' you're trying to horn-waggle me, boy, so I want you to know that you ain't foolin' this old coon. I see what you're up to, and you've made your point. I reckon there ain't no use in me tryin' to talk any dan' sense into your head, so since you're bound and determined to jump into this ruckus, welcome to the party of the Sweet Lady fools.' Then he extended his work-gnarled hand to shake.

They didn't pump hands but once, as it was more like a pledge between them, a personal reaching out between family who were actually strangers to each other, except for the bond of their common blood. Then they sat back, and Clint began to give Uncle Jeff all the news from home, though it'd been three years since he'd been there himself.

Intermittently, Uncle Jeff got up and filled cups with strong, hot coffee as they talked of family for an hour or more. Finally, after all the news was imparted, questions asked and answered, Uncle Jeff got up and went to the back of the shack. He reached down and pulled open a trap door about nine feet square.

Clint had noticed the cabin's arrangements curiously. In the center of the room, the timbers which held up the roof were larger than the rest of them. Then in the back of the room, right over the trap door, there was a block and tackle rigged up with a rope leading to what appeared to be a heavy platform leaning against the back wall. It was then that Clint realized why he hadn't seen any sign of a mine shaft or tunnel outside the shack. Uncle Jeff had built the stone shack over the top of the shaft.

'Come on, boy,' Uncle Jeff said, motioning for him. 'Let me show you what all this ruckus is 'bout, and let you feast your eyes on the most beautiful sight that God ever created for man to see.'

Clint got up from the table and walked over to the black opening just as Uncle Jeff tipped over the platform and straightened the ropes which held it at the four corners. The platform swayed recklessly over the hole in the cabin's floor.

Getting on the platform, Uncle Jeff

motioned for Clint to join him, then ordered Moses to guard the shack while they went down into the mine.

'Stay Moses. Watch!' Uncle Jeff said, and the wolf looked like he understood every word. But from the way Moses looked at Clint, he knew that the wolf had just written down another score against him in his book, which would have to be settled.

With a sigh, Clint stepped onto the platform and held two of the supporting ropes while Uncle Jeff shifted his weight to steady it and guide their descent with the block and tackle.

Just the rocking motion of the platform was enough to give Clint second thoughts, but when that black hole closed over them as Uncle Jeff began lowering the platform down into the mine, Clint knew right then he would never have to worry about being a miner. The deeper they went, the more Clint thought about all the nice solid ground above with the fresh air and stars shining overhead.

The platform didn't appear to be as well constructed as he thought it should be. But that might have been because it seemed awfully springy, and the way it kept swinging back and forth, hitting and scraping the rock walls as it went down into the damp, cold earth. The smell around him didn't help much either. It was like earth, rock, gunpowder, and wetness. Coupled with the total blackness, it gave a man a closed-in feeling. It didn't help to look up at the small square of light above, which grew smaller by the second. Soon the ropes started looking like strings to Clint; a mighty fragile lifeline for two men to be suspended by. The experience was frightening to a man who had never been down in a mine before, and Clint drew a deep breath to control the wild panic he momentarily felt.

After what seemed like hours of standing on the flimsy contraption, Uncle Jeff stopped it and stepped off into the pitch blackness. Taking Clint by the arm, he guided him into a low tunnel that had been blasted in the face of the shaft.

'Watch your head,' Uncle Jeff said warningly. 'It's kind'a low.'

And it was, being about five-feet high in most places. They proceeded for a short distance and stopped in a small, higher opening.

'Let's hold it here a minute, boy, while I

get us a light goin'. Then we can see what we're doin',' Uncle Jeff said, and added: 'I never brin' a lamp down on the elevator. Too shaky.'

He released Clint's arm while fumbling with something in the darkness. Clint immediately straightened up as Uncle Jeff said warningly: 'Watch your head, boy; there's low crossbeams in here.' But the warning came a moment too late, and Clint knew he'd have a bump on his head come morning.

'Thanks!' Clint said sarcastically, sorry he'd allowed himself to be enticed into entering the black pit.

'Don't mention it,' Uncle Jeff replied with a soft chuckle, knowing the word of warning had come too late. He'd momentarily forgotten that his own head just did pass under the beams, and Clint was considerably taller.

Just as the pain in Clint's head settled down to a dull throb, Uncle Jeff lit a match and touched it to the wicks of two candles. After the candles had sputtered to life, he handed one to Clint, so he could take a look at his surroundings.

It wasn't a comforting sight. The tunnel, running through the small workroom, was

101

about six feet high and four feet wide. The room was only slightly wider, with numerous hand tools leaning against the wall, and a large wheelbarrow used to haul rock to the elevator shaft. Cases of dynamite and small kegs of blasting powder were stacked up along one wall, and set upon a wooden platform to keep them out of the water lying in shallow pools on the rock floor.

The whole place, including the shafts, seemed to be gouged out of solid granite. The walls, floors, and ceiling glistened wetly, and water was dripping audibly all around them. The mine tunnel looked dark and forbidding; even worse than in the total darkness.

'Well, let's go, boy. This ain't nothin' here,' Uncle Jeff said, and took the lead as he crouched down low to keep from bumping his head on the low cross beams.

Clint saw that if the tunnels had been made higher or wider, it would have only meant more rock to haul to the surface. There were a few probing shafts which sniffed out the veins of gold, or gold-bearing ore.

He followed silently behind Uncle Jeff through the narrow tunnel for perhaps three full minutes, then suddenly it ended, and opened into a small, cavelike room about as big as a large closet, or a small bedroom.

Even in the dim light, the sight of what he beheld in the room was enough to make a man's heart stop beating. Clint forgot about being underground, and everything else, as his eyes focused on the breathtaking sight.

CHAPTER SIX

Gold! It was the kind of gold rarely seen outside of a placer mine, because it was almost pure.

Hard rock miners rarely saw real gold, as most of it is scattered in rock that has to be crushed in a stamp-mill, then the gold is extracted. Normally there might be only an ounce or two of gold to a ton in high-grade ore.

A round of powder had broken into the small cave, called a vug, and it was literally lined with gold. The vug was about eight feet high, six feet wide, and five feet long, but the ore, real high-grade in a find like this, extended far out into the walls, floor, and roof for a considerable distance.

Quartz and calcite crystals studded the wall, floor, and ceiling of the cave, and everywhere among them were thumbnail-size pieces of gold shining brilliantly in the flickering light of the candles.

Uncle Jeff had been scraping on those walls for almost a month, using, of all things, a gardener's hoe. He'd worked alone, scraping the walls, then chipping and crushing the rock crystals to separate the gold. Gold like this is never put through a stamp-mill, even in a big operation. It's usually cleaned and smelted on the spot, or sold, unprocessed, to the United States Mint.

Such a pocket of gold is very rare, and when one is found, it's usually called a 'jewelry shop,' 'high-grader's heaven' or 'Aladdin's Cave,' but Aladdin never saw the likes of it.

For several minutes, neither man said a word. Both were thinking of the wonder of the vug and the incredible luck in finding it.

Finally, Uncle Jeff spoke quietly with a furious pride in his hushed voice: 'Sure is a sight, ain't it, boy? I done struck it rich when I hit this bugger.'

'You surely did, Uncle Jeff,' Clint replied, matching the old man's hushed tone. 'Does anyone know what you've found here?'

'Nope, I ain't told nobody,' he replied quietly. 'Been penned up in here for quite a spell. Old Mark knew I was onto high-grade, and so did the assayer for that matter, but I managed to water down the samples I sent out. Yep, I knew I was on the track of high-grade with the shaft, but nothin' like this. Why, boy, it plum staggers the imagination what a vug like this is worth. Just workin' alone, I can scrape a fortune in gold right from these walls, then I can mine the high-grade for all it's worth. Yep, I figure this mine is worth a million dollars for sure.' The satisfaction in Uncle Jeff's voice left Clint with no reason to doubt. A million dollars!

Such a sum of money did stagger the imagination. It was unreal; like a dream, beyond the wildest dreams Clint had ever had. Then Clint realized how the gold had momentarily affected his thinking, and he grinned ruefully. It wasn't his. It was his Uncle Jeff's. Clint looked at the old man's face, and it shined with pride as he examined his treasure.

'Yep, you're right, Uncle Jeff,' Clint said quietly. 'If'n anybody knew what you had here, they'd stampede over you like a herd of loco cattle tryin' to get it away from you.'

'You're right 'bout it, boy,' he replied seriously. 'That's why I've been keepin' my mouth shut, and I intend to work it by myself. If'n I could go full time, I could get all this jewelry rock outta here, then brin' in a crew to mine the rest of the ore. Boy, you know, if'n there's one vug like this, there just might be 'nother one 'round.'

The possibility had occurred to Clint, too, although two such finds were rare. He couldn't remember hearing about two such caves ever found in one mine, but anything was possible.

Taking a short-handled pick from against the wall, Uncle Jeff tapped the rock face and dislodged a chunk of gold-bearing rock and handed it to Clint.

'Here, boy, take this for a good-luck piece. There ain't nothin' like gold to keep a man's pocket warm and cozy,' he said with a chuckle.

Clint examined the chunk of quartz crystal in the light of the candle. It was colored purple by the fluorides and had pure calcite crystals imbedded in a thumb-size piece of solid gold that weighed at least an ounce. It was rough and felt pleasantly warm in the palm of Clint's hand.

'Thanks, Uncle Jeff. I'll save it for a keepsake to remember this place by,' Clint said, then slipped the chunk of gold in his pocket.'Let's get outta here a'fore I get to thinkin' that Silk Barrister might not be so crazy after all. It ain't natural for a man that's never seen more'n a few dollars at a time to be tempted by such a sight. It sure takes a bit of gettin' use to.'

'I see your point, boy,' Uncle Jeff agreed, then turned to lead the way into the narrow mouth of the tunnel. As they progressed, Uncle Jeff said: 'Yep, it still seems mighty unreal to me at times.'

A few minutes later they were back on the surface, sitting at the table inside the shack, ready to decide what their next course of action would be. One thing was for sure: the presence of the vug would have to remain a closely guarded secret until it was worked, and the gold taken to a safe place and sold to the United States Mint in Denver.

If Silk Barrister ever made a real effort to take possession of the mine, he would be able to buy the support of crooked judges and politicians, and that would be the end of it. It had happened in other mining towns and it could easily happen in lawless Pine Creek.

If Barrister got his hands on the gold in the vug, he would be able to vastly increase his power by hiring whole armies of gunmen to support him. And Silk Barrister was already making a huge effort based just on the assayer's reports of the possibilities of high-grade ore in the vicinity. What would the skunk do if the extent of the strike leaked out? Plenty!

Uncle Jeff refilled Clint's cup with hot coffee and gave him a sharp look as he asked: 'Boy, you got any ideas?'

'Uncle Jeff, I'm kind'a a direct person, and 'bout the only way I know to take care of the problem is head on, then let the devil take the consequences. The only thin' I can see to do would be plant Silk Barrister and his bunch of skunks in boot hill to rid the world of their stink. But, you got this mine to think of, and a bloodbath ain't goin' to make it any easier on you. Since you got the most to lose, what do you think?'

The old man considered this for a minute before he spoke, and Clint could tell that

Uncle Jeff had been deliberating on the matter for a while.

'Boy, I ain't gonna lie to you,' he said briefly. 'It purely does gall me to be penned up in this shack while a bunch of polecats take potshots at me. But, I ain't no gunfighter like Silk Barrister's done went and hired for himself, so I'm kind'a stuck.'

He paused for a minute, lit up the clay pipe, and continued speaking: 'But, if'n I'm stuck in here, then so're they. I can't get out, but they can't get in. The closest they can get to me is the pile of timbers between here and the Fancy Nance, 'cause I got a good field of fire everywhere else. 'Sides that, I ain't gonna leave the mine and give 'em snakes a chance to get in.'

Uncle Jeff paused again and sat in thought for a minute. Then he said: 'If'n I had me a load of supplies and water, I could hole up here for quite a spell, and with a little help, I could work the vug for all it's worth. With the two of us—one watchin' and the other one workin'—why, we could clean out the vug inside a couple of weeks.'

'Yep,' Clint agreed, 'and we'd still be in the same shape, except both of us would be stuck in this trap. Nope, your idea don't seem too smart to me.

'The way I see it,' Clint continued before the old man could say anything, 'your first problem is to get some grub and water in, so if'n anythin' happens, then you can hold out. Since Barrister and his crew don't know 'bout me yet, I can take care of the chore right away. Then with me outside and you in here, why, we'll have those skunks caught between a rock and a hard place, and not the other way 'round.'

'Boy, you got a head on your shoulders, sure 'nuff. Now would be the perfect time to do it, since you've run those polecats of Silk's off. You could pick up a big load of supplies from the tradin' post. Barrister owns it, but he keeps a man in there all the time. If'n you're gonna do it, then you'll need a stake in your poke to get 'em supplies with,' Uncle Jeff said, as he got up from the table and walked over to where three fifty-pound powder kegs lined the wall of the shack.

He took a prize-bar in his hands and pried the top off one of the kegs of powder, then turned to Clint and said: 'Come over here and brin' one of those plates with you.'

Clint got up and picked up a tin plate from the table and crossed the room to his uncle's side. As he looked into the keg, his eyes widened in astonishment. The powder keg was brim full of gold nuggets.

'Yep,' Uncle Jeff said with a chuckle, 'I know what you're thinkin', boy, and you're right. All 'em kegs is plum full of gold. I reckon there's enough right there to let a man do just 'about anythin' he wanted to, and that's just surface scratchin'.'

'It's sure a sight of gold, Uncle Jeff,' Clint said softly.

'Boy, it's just a start,' he replied. 'The problem is to keep Silk's hands off the Sweet Lady and let her be worked like she oughtta be.'

Using the plate, Uncle Jeff scooped up a big pile of gold nuggets from the keg and carried it over to the table. After getting a leather pouch with draw strings on it, he filled it with the gold and tied off the top tightly. He handed it to Clint and went back to close the top on the keg.

Clint hefted the heavy pouch in his hand and judged its weight to be about six pounds. It was more money than he'd ever held in his hands before; near two thousand dollars worth of gold. Regretfully, Clint tossed the heavy pouch back on the table, then locked eyes with Uncle Jeff, who'd returned to stand by the table.

'Nope, we can't spend it, Uncle Jeff. It'll tip our hand for sure,' he said quietly, and asked: 'Have you got any cash money on hand?'

'No, boy, every dadburn cent I got is sunk in this mine. Ain't this somethin'. A million dollars in gold, and I can't even buy a can of beans,' Uncle Jeff said, then grinned mirthlessly into his beard, his gray eyes bleak.

'What 'bout Mark Tollett? Think he's got some cash salted away?' Clint asked. Uncle Jeff's face lit up momentarily, then faded.

'Yep, I reckon,' he admitted grudgingly, 'but I ain't askin' him for any.' His eyes glittered hard and flinty with pride, and Clint didn't miss the finality in his words. He wouldn't ask for a thing, even though he could pay it back a thousand times over.

'Uncle Jeff, I've got a hundred and fifty in coin, but it's not goin' to be enough; not with the prices the way they are 'round here. I figure we'll need another hundred or so at least. Now, thin' is, we could use Tollett for kind'a a bank; leavin' the gold with him as security against some coin and paper money. Now, ain't that reasonable? Besides, I'll be doin' the askin', not you.'

'Suit yourself,' Uncle Jeff said sharply; but relief was evident in his voice, and he was thankful his nephew had shown him a way round his stubborn pride.

'Uncle Jeff, I reckon you'll know it's me when I come back, 'cause I'll be usin' one of Tollett's wagons, but we'd better have us a signal just in case they catch onto us.'

He thought for a minute, then said: 'I was trackin' Apaches down in Arizona and they were good at soundin' like mornin' doves, and I got pretty good at it myself. I don't reckon Barrister's crew would think of mornin' doves up here in the high country,' Clint said with a smile.

Uncle Jeff nodded his head approvingly as a grin broke through his beard, then he said: 'Apaches always were slippery. I reckon it might be a mite unhealthy if'n a man was to pay me a call without bringin' one of 'em doves with him, seein' as how I've always been right partial to the little critters.'

Moses stood nearby and gave Clint a distrustful look as Uncle Jeff unbarred the door. But instead of opening it, he went back to the table and spoke to Clint from there.

'Boy, when I douse the light, let yourself

out real quick. No sense in givin' 'em a target to shoot at if'n they're out there,' he said quietly, then asked: 'You ready, boy?'

Clint put his hand on the wooden handle of the door and looked back at his uncle. A deep look of understanding passed between them in the brief second. 'Any time, Uncle Jeff,' he said softly.

A puff of breath into the chimney of the lantern plunged the cabin into darkness. Within a second, Clint was out the door, closing it softly behind him. Then he stood motionless in the deep shadow of the overhanging roof and waited expectantly for a shot which never came.

Breathing a sigh of relief, he let his eyes adjust to the darkness, then he moved into the night. He kept to the dark patches of the land and didn't show himself against the bare sections of gray rock lying exposed to the moonlight that still broke through the cloud cover.

Clint was glad he had forced the stake-out man to leave. If the man were still there, then there would have been a fusillade of bullets to greet Clint as he emerged from the shack. Instead, he was able to concentrate on getting to Tollett's stable where he could get a wagon to carry supplies back to Uncle Jeff, and borrow some money from Tollett, if he had any.

It was almost midnight. Clint knew he would have to hurry before Barrister and his bunch found out what was happening. It wouldn't take them long to fit the pieces together once they found out about the missing guard and the supplies that Clint expected to buy at Silk's Trading Post.

He was under no illusions about the kind of reaction Barrister would have when he found out about tonight's doings. Already Clint had put three of Barrister's men out of the picture; the two at Joe's, and the stake-out man. If nothing else, it was a fair night's work. Barrister wouldn't take kindly to it, and if Clint did manage to get in a wagon-load of supplies, then it would really rile Barrister up.

If Clint got the supplies, Pine Creek was going to become a mightly unhealthy place for him unless he managed to deal himself some high cards in the game. Clint wondered where he was going to get the aces he was going to be needing. It was one thing to declare war on someone, and quite another thing to fight the war; especially without a plan of battle, and he didn't have a clue as to what his next moves were going to be. He always took things a step at a time, and for now, there was the business of the supplies to worry him. When that was taken care of, he'd figure out something else.

Upon reaching the stables, Clint waited a moment before going in. He watched the building carefully to make sure there wasn't a reception committee waiting for him. Clint didn't expect any trouble this early in the game, but he hadn't reached the ripe old age of thirty by being careless.

Satisfied that everything was as it should be, he eased open the back door of the stable and slipped inside, only to suddenly feel the solidness of a double-barreled shotgun press into his back. He froze instantly, tensing himself for action, when Tollett's voice came from behind him.

'Sorry 'bout that, youngster,' he said with a dry chuckle. 'I wasn't rightly expectin' you back so quick, seein' as how I didn't hear no shootin' goin' on out north of town. Then a while back a skunk of Silk's came arunnin' in here aholdin' up his britches like he wasn't goin' to make it to the outhouse, so I figured you'd visit with your uncle for a while longer.'

'Mark, you're beginnin' to put a cramp

116

in my style by comin' up behind me like that. It's downright upsettin' to a man who ain't used to it,' Clint said, moving away from the barrels of the shotgun.

'Wish I could take credit for it, but I don't reckon it'd be right 'cause you're 'bout the quietest movin' youn' feller I ever did see. I'm pretty good at watchin' critters, though, and 'em mules smelled you right off,' Mark explained and chuckled.

Clint smiled ruefully to himself at the old man's shrewdness, and was glad to learn he wasn't slipping up in his old age, or getting careless. Turning to face Tollett in the dim light, he asked: 'What 'bout the feller who came in?'

'Acted right queer, the feller did,' Mark replied gleefully. 'He appeared to be in an awful hurry to get outta here. Seemed right shook up too; like he'd ran into a ghost or somethin' of the sort.'

After another chuckle, Mark explained, 'He came in and saddled his horse and left without sayin' a word. Last I saw of him, he was givin' some spur to the horse and headin' south. You wouldn't by any chance know why he was in such a hurry to travel, would you, youngster?'

'Someone must've convinced him that Pine Creek wasn't a very healthy place to be right now. Awful good place to catch a fatal disease, Pine Creek is,' he replied quietly.

'Yep, and I bet I know who convinced him of it. Since you've come to town, there seems to be a whole plague goin' 'round.'

'We'll see if it can't spread some more,' Clint said.

'Well, how's old Jeff makin' out?'

'He's holdin' out, Mark. I want to talk to you 'bout it,' Clint said seriously, then told him of their problems and needs as the old man listened intently.

'Come on and let's hook up a team,' Mark said when Clint finished talking.

As they hooked two big Missouri mules together to a wide-rimmed freight wagon, Tollett told him the McDonald kids were bedded down in his tack-room, and he was sleeping in the loft.

After the mules were hooked up and ready to go, Clint told Mark about the money situation and handed him the sack of gold nuggets as he said: 'Mark, we'd like to use this to borrow what cash you have on hand. There is 'bout two thousand in gold in this poke.'

'Youngster, I'll lend you and old Jeff all I

got, which ain't much; only a couple hundred dollars. But I don't want your gold for security,' he protested.

'Mark, I can't lug it around with me, so how 'bout holdin' on to it for Uncle Jeff 'till later on.'

'Yep, I can do it all right,' he agreed, then took the pouch of gold and went to his hiding place in the feed room. He returned within a few minutes with a small bundle of paper money and coins. 'Two hundred and forty dollars,' he said, handing it to Clint. 'Least it was the last time I counted it.'

'That's what it is then,' Clint replied, and put the money into his own poke, then tucked it behind his belt and climbed into the wagon seat. 'Well, it's time for Mr. Silk Barrister to sell me some groceries.'

'Youngster, Silk's goin' to bust a gut when he finds out he's sold supplies to old Jeff. Yes sirree, I'd give a month's profit to see his face when he finds it out,' Mark said, chuckling gleefully.

'I ain't got 'em groceries, yet,' Clint replied soberly. 'But if'n I get 'em, I hope he chokes on the profit he makes outta it.'

He slapped the rumps of the mules with the reins and started toward the front door of the stable, with Tollett going ahead to open the doors.

'Be careful,' Mark called as Clint drove the wagon into the muddy street and turned south toward the business district, such as it was, of Pine Creek.

He noticed that it hadn't gotten any quieter from the time he'd ridden into town that evening. If anything, it was worse. There were more drunken miners staggering in the street. The music seemed noisier as it blended with the loud laughter and the high squeals of the dance-hall girls. Occasional gun-shots exploded into the air. Clint knew that things would get even worse before it began to quiet down about three or four o'clock in the morning.

No one appeared to notice him, or even paid any attention as he drove the wagon down the muddy street. Everybody was too busy with their own enjoyments to pay any mind to a freight wagon and two mules being driven by a ragtail man with a heavy beard. This suited Clint just fine. He didn't want any attention focused on him anyway.

The sign of the Pine Creek Trading Post, J. Barrister, proprietor, loomed up a little south of the center of town. At first it looked as though there might not be anyone there, as the front door was closed and barred, and little light was visible from inside the store.

Then Clint spotted a column of smoke coming from a stovepipe at the rear of the building. Looking closer, he saw a light shining brightly in a rear window of the building. It was the living quarters of the man Barrister had hired to run the store.

Turning the mules into the dark alley beside the building, Clint turned again at the corner of the building and came opposite a door set above a loading dock in the rear. He pulled up the mules and set the brake, then wrapped the lines around the brake-handle and stepped off the wagon onto the loading dock.

The building was built of pine logs set horizontally and chinked with clay. It appeared to be one of the most solidly built buildings in town, and was also the largest, running about sixty feet by forty feet, which made it even larger than Tollett's stable.

The building contradicted everything that Clint had ever heard about Silk Barrister, who had never put roots down anywhere. He was the quick-money type, and never owned anything which might be there when he got out. So owning a building like this meant that Silk planned to stay for awhile. It looked as though Silk was changing his tactics in Pine Creek; posing as a legitimate businessman and pillar-of-the-community type, which might complicate Clint's usual, cold-blooded method of settling disputes.

Clint walked up to the solid-looking door and knocked. Getting no response from inside, he tried the door and found it locked, so he knocked again, much louder.

'Go away, we're closed,' a man called from inside the building.

Clint knocked again with more enthusiasm, and heard footsteps coming toward the door.

'I said, we're closed,' the man called again. 'Come back in the morning.' The man's voice sounded both exasperated and suspicious.

'Well, I figured that you'd make an exception in my case, seein' as how Mr. Barrister might get all upset if'n he knew I was here and what I've come for,' Clint called loudly through the door. 'Of course, if'n you'd rather I went and fetched him to let me in, then I guess I can do it, but I don't believe he'll like it very much.'

'Mr. Barrister didn't tell me anything

about you or anyone else coming around here after closing time, Mister, so I don't think I'd better let you in. How do I know you're not a robber?'

'I've never heard tell of a robber with a wagon and two mules before. But, never mind, I'll just go and get Mr. Barrister. You can explain to him why he had to get up in the middle of the night and come over here. I Don't think he's gonna like it very much,' Clint called in a regretful voice, stomping his boots loudly as though he was walking away.

'Wait a minute,' the man called loudly. 'Look, there isn't any need of getting Mr. Barrister. Tell me who you are and what your business is. Then maybe I can help you myself.'

'My name's Clint Jackson,' he called, making a show of returning to the closed door. 'I'm here to get a quick wagonload of supplies to take to the mine.'

'Mine! What mine?'

'Look, if Mr. Barrister ain't told you 'bout his business, then it ain't my place to do it; but this is pretty important to him.'

'You're picking up supplies for the Sweet Lady?'

'That's it,' Clint answered, tongue in

123

cheek.

'Why didn't you say so,' the man called. 'No need in getting Mr. Barrister. Let me get this door unbarred.'

The storekeeper was so elated that the boss's plans to take over the Sweet Lady mine had come true, he didn't question letting someone into the store to supply the mine. So he hurriedly unbarred the heavy door.

'Now you've got your heart in the right place,' Clint said, pushing his way into the store through the crack in the partly open door. 'I'll be sure to tell Silk how nice you were whenever I see him.'

In the back of the building was a rolltop desk with papers scattered over it, and a smoky lamp with a wick that needed trimming. A new swivel chair was in front of the desk. Through an open door, Clint could see a bed and figured it was the sleeping quarters for the man.

Turning to the storekeeper, he saw a shortish man who was overweight from soft living. He had a balding head and wore wire-rim glasses which were perched halfway down his shining nose.

He peered at Clint, noting with distaste and alarm the disheveled appearance of the big man he'd admitted into the store.

After rebolting the door, the man gave a sickly smile and looked at Clint with a pleading expression over the tops of his glasses.

'Let's see what you got that I can use,' Clint said, indicating the front of the store with a quick motion of his head and eyes.

The small, fat storekeeper drew a deep breath and led the way into the front of the store. Clint knew the man was going to be in a world of trouble when Silk found out about all the supplies he had sold—and to whom.

It wasn't that he'd told the storekeeper a lie. He just neglected to tell him more than he figured the man ought to know. It wasn't his fault the man thought he was working for Silk.

With a wide grin on his face and a light shining in his gray eyes, Clint began selecting a long line of items from the shelves of the store. Beans, rice, coffee, sugar, flour, canned stuff, ammunition, and the like. It began to pile up in a nice heap, and the man was too busy figuring up the prices to notice the size of Clint's smile. This was going to turn out mighty fine, Clint thought in satisfaction as he moved between the shelves and the piled counter.

CHAPTER SEVEN

When Silk Barrister stepped out of his cabin, located at the edge of town, he inhaled deeply, filling his lungs with the crisp morning air. The bright morning sunshine topping the mountain peaks fell directly upon his face, adding to his good feelings.

More often than not, Silk met the days with a kind of satisfied joy. The dreams of a lifetime, that of being rich and powerful, were coming to fulfillment. Soon he would be as rich and powerful as the Mellins, Morgans, and the Vanderbilts, then he would be able to taste the luscious pleasures the world had to offer the rich. He was very close to having it all, and nothing could stop him now. Nothing!

Turning north, he started walking along the wide boards that had been laid over the muddy ground toward the center of town. Pine Creek appeared dull and drab under the bright sunshine, a scabrous, brown eyesore set in the bottom of what once had been a beautiful mountain meadow between rising ridges of the Rocky Mountains. But that was the way it always was when men sought the riches beneath the ground, tearing up everything that would impede their search. Everywhere on the ridges were stumps of trees that had been ruthlessly cut down for plank floors in tents, siding, and roofing for the dugouts, and, above all, for the rocker boxes used to separate the gold from the mud in the stream that bisected the meadow.

Placer mining was already a thing of the past. The gold taken from the stream was almost negligible, and the single-pan miners, whose equipment was a shovel, pan, and rocker box, were almost all gone now. That left the deep-tunnel mining to the big boys, the ones who had money to invest in workers and machinery. They bored deeply into the mountainside that seemed literally filled with gold-bearing ore.

Most of the deep mines were to the north of town and Silk now owned several of those mines. All of them looked promising, but presently they were barely paying expenses. He had yet to recoup the large amounts of cash he'd poured into the mines to get them going.

As he walked along, Silk noticed the early morning bustle as the town came awake and people recovered from the previous night. They went about their business with false smiles of respectability on their faces while, in their hearts, they burned with the greed that they all shared: gold fever.

Silk smiled to himself. He knew these men for what they were: a pack of ravenous wolves. But if they were wolves, then he was the pack leader; the strongest and smartest of all. Silk suppressed a dry chuckle as he thought of the gold that was already lining his own pockets, and not from the mining either. He secretly owned or controlled most of the business interests in Pine Creek, a source of income more certain than digging for gold.

Several dozen people saw Silk Barrister walking down the street, his fleshy face set with self-satisfaction. His face looked like greasy brown paper, and the expensive suit looked cheap and dowdy on his heavy frame. Once a powerful man with thick, muscular arms, chest, and shoulders, he was now soft and fleshy, his stomach swollen with fat as though an enormous malignant growth was growing within him.

Restless, constantly shifting black eyes looked out ruthlessly and contemptuously from under dark, thick brows, while a fleshy nose ended in slightly flared nostrils. A black, neatly trimmed mustache rode above full lips. His chin was lost in a mass of flesh that was pock-marked, as were his fat cheeks.

Silk noticed the stares the people turned his way, looks that were filled with various degrees of fear, loathing, and contempt, strangely mixed with a subtle eagerness to please, to ingratiate themselves with the power he represented; if only to be allowed to pursue their own fortunes out of his notice and concern. In the back of every look was respect for the power he held over the lives of every person in Pine Creek, and knowledge of his willingness to use it.

Silk recognized the looks for what they were, and it gave him a tremendous pleasure knowing he could command power over other men. If nothing else, he was a realist and saw things for what they were. He was also ruthless, and wouldn't hesitate to destroy anyone or anything that threatened the fulfillment of his dream.

He had learned early in his life that to get

what he wanted most—respect and power—it was necessary to become rich, and his best tool to achieve wealth was his brain. A man could use his brain to pry out the fears, secrets, and weaknesses of other people, then use the information for his own means. Ethics and morals were for the weak. To be successful, a man took what he wanted regardless of what anyone thought of his methods. Once a man had money and power, the methods he used to achieve it were no longer important.

As Silk neared the trading post, where he conducted most of his business, he paused for a minute when he saw a new, open-top carriage coming down the street toward him. It was pulled by a pair of matched bays, and it took Silk a moment to place the woman driving it. It was Shirley Claymore, the young wife of Will Claymore.

As she drew closer, Silk saw her milk-white skin and lovely blonde hair, which was piled up under a fashionable hat. Her long-sleeved, blue silk dress with its high lace collar did nothing to hide the perfection of her figure, or conceal the exquisite mounds of her breasts, which seemed ready to burst from the confining material of the dress. Her waist was small, but uncorseted, her back straight and proud. Her squared shoulders lifted the mounds that strained against the fabric of the dress.

Reluctantly, Silk raised his eyes to study the small oval face. It was highlighted by wide-spaced eyes and a pert, aristocratic nose, which tilted upward as though in disdain, and Silk thought: 'I'd like to humble that arrogant look of yours.'

Her lips were utterly sensuous, full and wide, tinted with a pink color that was scandalous even on a respectably married woman. Silk felt his breathing grow heavier and his palms becoming cold and damp with sweat from the sight of her.

'Pure class,' he thought, and wondered how that old fool, Will Claymore, had managed to get such a young and beautiful woman to marry him. This was the first time that Silk had seen Claymore's young wife, but he knew who she was from the descriptions he had heard. Other men said that she was beautiful, but the descriptions of her beauty didn't do her justice. Her presence heightened her natural attractions, and brought them to a perfect whole.

When the carriage drew near, she

suddenly turned her head Silk's way and startled him with the boldness of her look. Her deep blue eyes locked for a second on Silk's dark ones, and her full, sensuous lips moved into a half smile accompanied by a slight nod of her lovely head. Then, just as quickly, she turned her face away as Silk hastily tipped his hat. The carriage swept past and continued on down the street.

In the brief second when their eyes had locked, Silk thought he knew why Will Claymore had been able to get such a beautiful woman to marry him, then come west, when anyone would have thought she would rather have stayed in the east with all its culture and refinement.

It had to be a marriage of convenience. Will Claymore and his brother, Paul, owned the Fancy Nance mine that was pouring a steady stream of wealth into their pockets now that financing had been arranged to bring in heavy equipment and hire big crews to dig out the gold ore.

Right after the two Claymore brothers struck promising color in the Fancy Nance, Will Claymore had gone east to find financial backing based upon the assayer's reports, while his younger brother stayed behind to work the mine and watch over their ranch. Will returned with more than just financing for the mine. The fifty-four-year-old rancher and mine owner returned with a bride young enough to be his daughter, and beautiful enough to cause a falling out between the two brothers.

Paul Claymore had been heard to curse Will for being an old fool, and, privately, Silk agreed. It was obvious why Shirley had married Will, and if Silk could see it, so could everybody else, including Paul.

She did have her points, though. It was plain from the way she carried herself that she was a real lady, well-bred and finished in the best of young ladies' schools, according to the customs of the day.

Since she was obviously well-bred, and beautiful besides, why would she marry an old fool like Will Claymore when she could have married practically any rich man she desired, and stayed in the east? That was a puzzle, unless . . . unless she was as poor as a church mouse. That might explain it. Nobody wanted to get saddled with a church mouse and a church mouse's relatives. In the east and north, since the war, there were considerably more women than men, and the men could pick and choose.

The look she had given him had been as bold as brass, and was the last thing he'd expected. She had to know who he was and that he was trying to take over the Fancy Nance by fair means or foul.

If Silk could get control of the Fancy Nance, he would be set. The Fancy Nance was actually two mines in one, as the Claymore brothers had filed side by side claims. The Claymores had played it cagey and said nothing to anyone until they were sure that they had located the source of the placer gold they'd discovered. When they finally filed their claims, the gold rush was on.

It had been the smartest thing to do. Paul Claymore had discovered the presence of rough grains of gold in the stream bed, and told his brother. Then, together, they had panned northward until they found the runoff stream that was carrying the gold into the meadow stream that ran through Pine Creek valley. Once they found the place where the gold originated, they brought in a geologist and filed their claims side by side in the most promising spot.

Silk knew that the Claymores were beginning to get rich. His own mine, the Vindicator, just above the Fancy Nance, was showing good color and yielding about an ounce a ton. It was starting to make expenses.

That was why Silk was putting so much pressure on Jeff Pickens, who had the mine below the Fancy Nance claims. If Silk could get his hands on the Sweet Lady, he would have the Claymores caught between the Vindicator and the Sweet Lady, and could squeeze the Claymores out of business. But old Jeff was putting up more resistance than Silk thought was possible. Silk was determined to put a stop to that right away; he was tired of waiting.

Turning into the alley that ran between the trading post and the saloon next door, which he secretly owned, he came to a sudden halt and looked down at the ground with a puzzled expression.

Wagon tracks, and fresh ones at that. Looking at them, he knew they were the wide tracks of a freight wagon and had been made after he'd left the night before. He followed the deep cuts all the way to the back door of his office, where they ran by the loading dock. One look at the tracks showed that the wagon had stood outside the store for some time and had left loaded.

Silk climbed the short flight of steps and

inserted his key into the lock on the door only to find it was already unlocked. He opened it and entered the back office.

He immediately knew that something was wrong. Cole Neyland, Chu'ta, and his bookkeeper and store manager, McSweeny, were all waiting in the office for him. Closing the door softly behind himself, he gave them all a slow look, then walked over to the rolltop desk and sat down in the swivel chair, turning to face the three men.

'Well?' Silk said questioningly, looking at each one of the men.

Cole Neyland was the first to speak. He was leaning against the back wall; the straight-back chair he was in tipped in a precarious position. He was dressed in a black, broadcloth suit, white shirt, gray vest, and black string tie. His flat-crowned, narrow-brimmed, gambler's style hat was tilted back on his head, and the guns he wore under the coat bulged prominently.

Neyland glanced over at Chu'ta, who was slumped against the opposite wall, seemingly uninterested in what was going on around him. Then he glanced over at McSweeny, who was clearly nervous.

Looking Silk directly in the eyes, Cole

said slowly, pronouncing the words clearly in a mellow tone of voice: 'We have some trouble, Silk.'

'What is it this time?' Silk asked in a suddenly tired voice, looking away from the cold, smoky gray eyes of Neyland.

'You won't like it,' Cole replied. 'Last night at Joe's, Bert and Nails tangled with a cowboy. A drifter in town, or so I thought until this morning. Bert and Nails came out second best with the drifter. He nearly killed both of them, and he wasn't even trying to.'

'How bad are they?' Silk asked quietly. Not that he really cared, as they were just two tools that he used to gain what he wanted out of life.

'Pretty bad, so I have been told. I believe that Bert will survive. The doctor said Bert's stomach is tore up and he will be deaf in one ear. The doctor is not so sure about Nails. They were having some fun with that little Irish girl Joe had working for him, and the drifter walked over both of them. He worked Bert over real good with a stick of firewood and a cigar, and the doctor cut two forty-four bullets out of Nails, The doctor said that Nails had a slim chance of pulling through, but that's about all.'

'Where were you when all this was happening?' Silk asked angrily. 'That's what I hired you for; to take care of trouble.'

'Sorry, Mr. Barrister, but that's not what you hired me for. I do not hire out to play nursemaid to the likes of those two, and I do not really give a damn what happens to them. Somebody is going to kill them sooner or later anyway; especially if they keep tangling with men like that drifter, Clint Jackson. I did not get to see him myself, but he gave his name to McSweeny, and I recognize his style. It fits with everything else that took place last night.'

'Cole, what are you talking about? What's everything else supposed to be?' Silk demanded in exasperation.

'Last night, after Clint Jackson finished with Bert and Nails and left Joe's with the two Irish kids, he ran off the new man you had watching the Sweet Lady. After that, he came down here with a freight wagon and bought enough supplies to outfit an army. This morning, Chu'ta trailed those wagon tracks to the Sweet Lady mine shack and back to Tollett's stables. When it went to the mine it was heavy, and when it returned it was empty. McSweeny has a list of everything that Jackson bought,' Cole said, finishing in the same mellow tone of voice.

Silk could feel the blood pounding in his temples as his anger rose. He silently looked at McSweeny, who was standing nervously in the doorway. McSweeny's face turned a chalky white as he felt the deadliness of Silk's cold, black eyes.

For a long minute, Silk was so mad that he couldn't trust himself to speak, but, with an effort, he bottled up his inner fury. When he finally broke the ensuing silence, it was with a voice of icy calmness.

'McSweeny, who told you to sell any supplies after I left last night?' Silk asked coldly.

'No-no one, M-Mr. Barrister,' he stammered.

'McSweeny, you're a damn fool, and if I didn't need you right now, I just might be inclined to make sure that you never make the same mistake again. You do understand me, don't you?'

'Y-yes s-sir,' he stammered nervously. 'I-I j-just thought . . .'

'Shut up, you damn idiot!' Silk roared as he finally lost control of his temper. Then he said in a cold, even voice: 'I don't want to hear any stupid excuses. You may have ruined my plans for taking over that mine. Give me the list so I can see how much damage you have done.'

Anxious to please and to get Silk's cold eyes looking elsewhere, McSweeny held the list out. Silk snatched it out of his hand and quickly began to scan it. After looking to see the quantity of the purchases, he started over and read the list slowly, letting the meaning of each purchase settle in his mind.

Foodstuffs, enough to feed an army for two months. Guns, two .44 caliber Colt Lightning pump-action rifles. Ammunition, two thousand rounds of .44 caliber and five hundred rounds of .50 caliber. Dynamite, one case with caps and fuses. Dry goods, six items. Eleven bear traps.

'Bear traps?' Silk asked, looking at McSweeny in puzzlement.

'Y-yes s-sir,' he stammered. 'He bought every one that we had in stock.'

'What in the hell would he want with bear traps?' Silk mumbled to himself. Everything else on the list made sense except that one purchase, and that's what worried him. When he couldn't understand something clearly, he automatically felt threatened. By looking at the list, he realized one thing: his present plans for taking over the Sweet Lady mine were ruined, so now he would have to find some other way.

Also, he felt that this Jackson character, whoever he was, could be very dangerous if he wasn't handled just right. 'Hell,' Silk thought, 'he disposed of three men in one night and broke the siege on the mine shack. That was a pretty fair night's work for any man.'

Having satisfied himself about the list, Silk laid it on the desk and turned to McSweeny, who was still standing nervously a few feet away. 'You better go open up for business before somebody starts wondering if anything is wrong,' Silk said in a mild tone of voice. 'Don't let anybody come back here until I'm finished. Do you think that you can do all that without me holding your hand?'

'Y-yes s-sir, Mr. Barrister,' he replied. As he was leaving, Silk stopped him.

'McSweeny, what did this Jackson use to pay for those supplies?' Silk asked, a glimmering of an idea taking shape in his mind.

'Cash, sir, all in coins and bills.'

'Cash?'

'Y-yes sir, on the barrelhead. Three hundred and ten dollars.'

'All right,' Silk said, disappointment in his voice as McSweeny left the room.

It had been an idea, but now the thought that the old man had struck a vein faded from his mind. Still, where had he gotten the money? Even before he had holed up in the stone shack he built for himself, the old man was hurting for ready cash, to Silk's delight. Now the old man had money to burn and had even hired a gunfighter to help him.

Then again, why would he bring in a gunfighter if there was nothing to protect in the mine? Silk didn't know, but he realized one thing: he would now have to take care of both the old man and the gunfighter.

Cole Neyland and Chu'ta hadn't moved while Silk was thinking about this latest development. Cole was still sitting with his chair tilted against the wall, calmly cleaning his fingernails with a small penknife. Chu'ta sat against the wall, looking at an invisible spot between his moccasined feet. He appeared not the slightest bit interested

142

in anything that had happened all morning. Then, as Silk spoke, they both looked at him.

'Cole, what do you know about this Clint Jackson?'

'Not too much,' Cole replied. 'He comes from Texas, and manages to get around quite a bit. He did some scouting for the army in Arizona against the Apaches.'

At those words, Chu'ta's head came up and his impassive dark eyes seemed to glow momentarily with a burning fire. Then they veiled over to show nothing.

'Later on,' Cole continued quietly, 'he rode shotgun for a stage line out of Fort Summer. The man has a small reputation of being a bad character to cross, but he does not look for trouble, and he is not a professional gunfighter that I know of.'

'Can you take him?' Silk asked.

'I have yet to meet the man that I cannot kill,' Cole replied evenly.

'Where is this Jackson now?'

'We don't know. Chu'ta believes that he left town this morning going north. At least that's what the signs indicated.'

'Now, why would he ride out of here going north? There isn't anything up that way except trees and mountains. Unless he has something else planned that we should know about,' Silk said thoughtfully.

'What are you going to do?' Cole asked mildly.

'I think we had better find out what this Clint Jackson is up to. Maybe we had better have a little talk with him and see if he will take more money than he is getting now. You and Chu'ta try to convince him of the good sense in joining up with me.'

'Silk, that is almost like asking a snake not to bite you. If you ask me, I don't like it,' Cole said evenly.

'I'm not asking you what you like, Cole. I'm telling you to do it,' Silk replied coldly.

'No,' Cole said flatly.

'What?' Silk asked, amazed at having his orders refused or questioned.

'I said no. I'm not riding up on him with a proposition from you. It would very likely come down to a shooting, and I get paid for each one of my killings; payment in advance, just as always,' Cole replied.

Silk was silent for a minute as he realized the wisdom of Cole's words. Jackson was already a proven enemy, so there was no use in talking to him. Better to just eliminate him and get it over with.

'All right, Cole,' Silk said quietly. 'Kill

him. Payment as usual.' Then, reaching in his desk, he brought out his cash box and counted out two piles of gold double eagles. One thousand dollars; five hundred apiece. Then he put the box back in the desk.

Both men stood up and walked over to the desk to get their money, then hefted the coins in their hands.

'Make sure that you do a good job,' Silk said evenly as he looked up at Cole.

'Don't worry, Silk,' he replied. 'You just bought another dead man.'

Cole and Chu'ta then turned and left the building, and Silk turned his attention to the next moves he needed to make against both the Fancy Nance and the Sweet Lady mines.

CHAPTER EIGHT

From a shelf of rock jutting out from the tree line of a nearby hillside just north and east of the mines of Pine Creek, Clint sat with his back against a smooth boulder and studied the mine workings through a pair of field glasses.

Dozens of miners had just arrived for the

day shift and were alighting from the ore wagons. They moved in clusters of threes and fours toward the dark openings of the mine shafts.

The side of the mountain where the mines were gleamed brightly in the morning sun. There wasn't a bush or tree to be seen on the rocky slopes near the mines. There were stark patches of evidence of the ruthlessness with which all the vegetation had been cut down and cleared away to be used in the buildings and mines, and for firewood.

Clint saw no sign of activity around the Sweet Lady, except for the spiral of smoke rising into the crisp morning air from the stovepipe. Otherwise, the place might have been a graveyard compared to the other mines.

He focused the glasses on the timber pile between the Sweet Lady and the Fancy Nance, but saw no flash of colors or movement indicating that the guard had been replaced. Not that it really made any difference now, because Uncle Jeff was set to hole up in the shack for as long as necessary. Clint smiled when he thought of the almost frantic activity of the past night when he'd delivered the wagonload of supplies to his uncle.

After leaving the trading post with the supplies, Clint had returned to Tollett's stable and they had filled several twenty-gallon water barrels to take to the mine. While Clint was gone, Uncle Jeff hadn't been idle. He'd spent his time preparing dynamite charges.

Working together, Uncle Jeff and Clint managed to get all the supplies up to the shack from the road. Once everything was inside the stout walls, they concealed several dynamite charges around the mine, most of which could be set off by a rifle shot. The pile of timbers laying between the Sweet Lady and the Fancy Nance was rigged to be set off with several long fuses, two of which were dummies. Clint smiled at the old man's devilishness, fixing a trap within a trap.

While Uncle Jeff was occupied, Clint set out the bear traps in places where a man might set his foot on the upward slope above the shack. Then he carefully concealed them with dirt and gravel. If anyone tried to get close to the shack from above to throw a dynamite charge onto the roof, they would be surprised at what awaited them.

Then, according to their agreement, Clint returned the wagon to Tollett, got his horse and left town headed north. After passing the turnoff to the mining area, he continued on, following the small creek and covering his trail in anticipation of being tracked. The Apache, Chu'ta would most likely be on his trail as soon as the game was known to Barrister, and Clint held no illusions about the ability of the Apache to follow the dimmest trail.

Clint had learned a lot in the years of hunting in Texas and scouting for the army, so he did a good job on his backtrail. He left the creek only after wrapping the roan's hoofs in burlap sacks, then came out on a rock shelf that a man wouldn't think a horse could climb. He was satisfied that his trail was pretty well obscured, and he was temporarily safe from pursuit.

Since there were no signs of anything unusual happening around the Sweet Lady, Clint moved away from the shelf and began climbing the steep slope behind him. After getting the roan, he followed a game trail due south to where he had made camp near a mountain run-off which led into the main creek. It was a pleasant glade, lightly treed with ash, elm, and fir alongside a stream that was only four or five feet wide.

Water fell from a higher shelf, cutting out a shallow pool. Although Clint was bone tired, he unsaddled Star so the roan could graze. Then he prepared himself a breakfast of pan bread, bacon, and beans, along with a pot of strong coffee.

After eating, he put a can of water on the fire to heat, and got out the straight razor Uncle Jeff had given him. He hung a piece of mirror on a tree and stropped the razor on his belt. With great reluctance, Clint applied the razor to the heavy winter beard, and when it was finally off, it left his face looking like a two-colored mask. He did feel almost civilized again, but awfully tender, like the skin on his face was new and raw.

Clint knew the pool was about five feet deep, since he had tested it with a pole, and that it was as cold as a blue norther. Now he debated whether or not to ease into the water gradually or jump in. He finally decided that shock treatment was the best way, and the most suited to his nature, as he slipped out of his dirty clothes.

He stood there on the edge of the pool naked as the day he was born, and clenched a bar of lye soap in his hand. Clint's body was lean through the shanks and hips, but broad and full in the chest and shoulders. His skin was so white that it looked unhealthy compared with the deep brown skin of his upper face, hands, and arms. But there was nothing unhealthy about the cords of muscle which flowed gracefully with a life and vitality all their own.

Taking a deep breath, Clint stepped back and looked toward the sky. Then, knowing that the man upstairs was probably taking pity on his foolish hide, he took a running step and hurled himself into the pool. The coldness of the water hit him like a bolt of lightning as it closed over his head. Instantly straightening his legs, he pushed himself off the bottom of the pool. Coming halfway out of the water, Clint let out a pent-up bellow, howling like a bull with his tail caught in a barn door. The shock of the cold water seemed to immobilize everything about him except his vocal cords.

His natural inclination was to jump out of the pool immediately, but with a great effort, he forced himself to stay in the water. With stiff movements, Clint began to soap himself. He watched his skin turn from red to blue as the blood left his outer skin, withdrawing deeper into his body for protection from the cold. He scrubbed vigorously, especially his long, thick hair, then took a deep breath and submerged again to rinse the soap from his head.

When he surfaced and began to move toward the bank of the pool, Clint was startled to hear a light, musical laugh, and looking toward the campfire, he saw a beautiful, blonde-haired woman standing by the fire with a wide smile on her tinted lips.

Clint had found himself in some pretty awkward situations in the past, but never one to equal this. Here he was, naked as a jaybird, and blue with cold, while a beautiful woman stood laughing at him, and she was between him and his clothes.

'Mister,' she said, laughing merrily, 'you're about the loudest man I've ever heard, and right now, the funniest one.'

'Ma'am, I don't know who you are, or how you came across my camp, but if'n you don't turn around so I can get outta this water a'fore I turn into a cake of ice, you're gonna see somethin' a lot more than funny,' Clint said through chattering teeth.

She blushed slightly. 'Certainly, sir,' she said with mocking humor and a curtsy. She turned her back and walked over to the campfire.

Clint was out of the pool in less than a minute. Then he vigorously rubbed his skin dry with a towsack. He quickly slipped on the new clothes he'd bought at Barrister's trading post, then pulled on his boots over new socks. With a quick movement, his gunbelt went around his waist and he buckled it low on his hips.

'Ma'am, you can turn around now,' he said, walking over to the fire. He squatted down beside it and held his hands over the fire to warm them.

When the woman turned around, Clint gave her a sharp look, noting her fashionable clothes and the full-bloomed figure that curved with the suggestiveness of youthful beauty. She bent down and filled a coffee cup from the pot and handed it to him.

'Here, drink this,' she ordered.

'Thank you,' Clint replied, accepting the cup with numb fingers, then sipping the hot brew. 'Lady, I'm a mite curious as to who you are and how you found my camp.'

She laughed lightly, then gracefully sank down on his saddle and said: 'That's easy enough. I'm Mrs. Will Claymore. Shirley to all my friends. And I was just driving by when I heard your yelling. So, I decided to see what could possibly be making such unearthly sounds.'

'Passin' by?' Clint asked, puzzled.

'Yes,' she replied, and saw his puzzled expression. 'On the road. It's just on the other side of those trees. Didn't you know it was there?'

'No ma'am, I rode in from the north early this mornin', but I'm much obliged to find it out.'

'The road goes from Pine Creek around these hills and into some mountain meadows. My husband has a ranch further up the road.'

'A ranch, ma'am?' Clint asked, even more puzzled. 'I thought that you might be the Claymores who own the Fancy Nance mine in Pine Creek.'

Shirley's eyes went cold, and shut him out of their clear, blue depths. A small movement of her hand to a pocket of the dress revealed that she went around armed with a pistol. She stared at him critically.

'My husband and his brother, Paul, own the Fancy Nance mine,' she said tonelessly, and added: 'They made the original strike in Pine Creek.'

'That's what I've heard,' Clint said. 'I just wondered about this ranch thin', that's all. I didn't know that Will Claymore was also a rancher.'

'Why are you interested in the Fancy Nance?' she asked evenly. 'And who are you anyway?'

'My handle is Clint Jackson, ma'am, and I ain't got any interest in the Fancy Nance,' he replied. 'I'm in Pine Creek on a little business of my own; family business.'

'I don't recall any Jacksons around here,' she said, slipping her hand into the dress pocket.

'Ma'am, you ain't goin' to be needin' that gun you've got in your pocket. You've got nothin' to worry 'bout with me. It might ease your mind somewhat to know my uncle's name is Jeff Pickens, and I've come to lend a hand in his troubles with the Sweet Lady mine.'

Her pretty face cleared immediately, but the hand remained in the pocket, and she said: 'Can you prove that?'

'Ma'am, I need to prove nothin' to you,' Clint answered quietly. 'What I'm doin' in Pine Creek ain't none of your concern.'

Shirley flushed and realized that somehow she'd injured his pride with her inquiry. Western men took a bit of getting use to, because they were not at all like the men in the east.

'I'm sorry if I offended you, Mr. Jackson,' she said softly. 'It's just if you're here to help your uncle, then you will be going up against the same gang of cutthroats who have made several attempts to kill my husband and his brother. You must know about Mr. Barrister and his hired gunmen.'

'I do,' Clint replied, 'and I'll fix their wagons for 'em the first chance I get.'

'Mr. Jackson, you sound as though you believe it will be an easy task. I assure you that it will not be. Barrister has hired some of the deadliest gunfighters he could find to assist him in his greedy designs.'

'Ma'am, I'm not sayin' that it's goin' to be easy, but when you take on a chore of cleanin' out a den of rattlesnakes, then you just do it and kill 'em a'fore they can bite you.'

'You sound as though you may be a gunfighter yourself, Mr. Jackson. You sure do have the look of one.'

'Ma'am, that mister kind'a sticks in my ear, and I'd rather you call me Clint, or even "hey you" rather'n that. I can't rightly help what I look like, but I don't consider myself a gunman. However, I do know how to use a gun when it needs usin'.'

'Clint, I believe you, and I think you're just the man to clean up Pine Creek. Every decent person will be grateful to you if you can do it. You can count on the Claymores for any help you might need.'

'What I can't understand is why you people have let the situation get like it is. The time to stop all the trouble was when it first started.'

'My husband tried to do just that, Clint, but every town marshal he hired has been gunned down in the streets, and now Barrister's bullies have all the men terrified. The mine owners are practically alone, since the workers distrust them anyway, and they are not about to risk their lives for someone else's interests. As soon as the independent placer miners left, Barrister and the others managed to breed distrust between the workers and the owners. It's a bad situation, and everybody is pretending to ignore what's going on.'

'That's the way of the world. When you've got somethin', you got to be ready to defend it,' Clint said quietly. 'It seems to me that if'n the mine owners themselves got together, they could run Barrister out.'

'Against professional gunmen? Surely you're not serious? There have already been several attempts on my husband's life, and Paul's too. But, thankfully, they are both careful men and have managed to avoid the traps that were set for them.'

'Why ain't your husband hired some gunfighters of his own?' Clint asked curiously.

'William is a very law-abiding man. He does not believe in hiring gunmen, and feels that to resort to those means would make the cure worse than the disease.'

'Yep,' he agreed, 'but when a forest fire is burnin', sometimes the only way to stop it is to make a fire of your own; one that you can control.'

'In other words, fight fire with fire?' Shirley asked, starting to understand what he was talking about.

'That's right.'

'Yes, I feel exactly the same way myself,' she replied, then regarded him respectfully. 'Have you been able to talk to your uncle yet?'

'Yes ma'am,' he answered, then he told her about the run-in at Joe's over the kids, his talk with his uncle, and buying the wagonload of supplies from the trading post. He said nothing about the traps laid around the Sweet Lady mine, but Shirley smiled outright about him buying the supplies.

'Mr. Barrister is not going to like what you have done, Clint,' she said with a twinkle in her blue eyes. 'But what are you going to do now? Have you got a plan?'

'No ma'am, I'm just kind'a playin' it by ear right now,' he admitted.

'Why don't you come by our ranch and have a talk with William? I'm sure that he would like to see you and would lend you assistance.'

'I don't see any reason why not. Where is your place?' Clint asked, liking the intelligence of Shirley and her friendly manner.

She gave him directions to the Claymore ranch, then she stood up, rising with an easy fluid grace.

'We'll be looking forward to seeing you at the ranch, Clint,' she said as he walked her through the trees to where her carriage and matched bays were standing on the narrow roadway.

'Are you goin' to be all right travelin'

around by yourself?' Clint asked, as he took her arm to assist her into the seat of the carriage.

'Certainly Clint,' she said with a light musical laugh. 'The ranch is only a few miles from here. Besides, I'm a very good shot with my pistol.'

'I believe it, ma'am.'

'Oh, yes,' she said brightly. 'When I next go into town, I will have a talk with Mary and ask her to come to work for me. Anything would be better than working in those saloons in town.'

'I'd be much obliged, ma'am.'

'Please, call me Shirley,' she said softly.

'All right Shirley,' he said.

She gave him a nod and a friendly smile, then flicked the reins to start the bays on their way, and Clint returned to his camp site.

CHAPTER NINE

Cole Neyland and the half-breed Apache, Chu'ta, stood motionless on the game trail above the small clearing where Clint had made his camp. A fire let only a trickle of smoke rise into the air, which was quickly disbursed by the leaves of the trees under whose branches it had been built.

'We will take him from two sides,' Cole said in a low voice.

Chu'ta, who was slightly ahead and thus in a better position to see directly into the camp, turned impassive black eyes on Neyland, and asked without emphasis: 'The woman too?'

'What?' Cole asked, nudging his horse up beside the Apache. The odor of feral, unwashed skin assaulted his nostrils.

Cole looked down into the camp and saw that Clint was facing a woman, who was seated on a saddle across the fire from him. He recognized her as Shirley Claymore, and wouldn't have been more surprised if it had been his own mother sitting with Jackson.

It was obvious to Cole that the two had met here in the hills to talk. Cole figured that the uppity Mrs. Claymore had sent for Jackson, and was using the situation with the Sweet Lady mine to hide the real reasons for Jackson's presence in the area.

'No,' Cole said thoughtfully. 'We had better not harm her. It would really get the Claymores' backs up, but when she leaves, we will take out Jackson. Chu'ta, work your way around to the other side of the camp, and I will edge closer from here. Take him at the first chance after the woman leaves.'

Chu'ta said nothing. He simply took the reins of his spotted mustang and nudged the horse into the woods to cross the stream above the waterfall and come in from the far side of the camp.

Cole also eased into the woodline and moved as carefully as possible. Then he tied his horse to a tree some distance from Jackson's camp. He slipped a new Marlin pump rifle from its saddle scabbard and automatically checked it over, simultaneously jacking a cartridge into the chamber and setting the safety catch. Cole disliked the woods and moved clumsily through them to a position close to the camp.

After crossing the small stream, Chu'ta left his own horse in a clearing some distance from Jackson's campsite. Unlike Cole, he slipped through the words like a shadow; silent and deadly as a coiled rattlesnake. In his hands, he carried an old cavalry carbine; a .45–.70 single shot. That didn't worry the half-breed, as he had never failed to make the first shot count.

As the two bushwhackers took up their positions, one on each side of the camp, Chu'ta, who had arrived first, was surprised to find the place deserted. He wondered if Jackson had heard Cole's approach through the woods, and was preparing to turn the tables on him.

Chu'ta cast his eyes around the enclosing trees and brush, and in doing so, he missed seeing Jackson return to the camp.

But Clint didn't fail to notice that the roan's ears were pointed directly toward the spot where Chu'ta lay waiting in ambush. Clint tensed, then took a slow breath to steady his nerves. He was caught in the open, and any indication that he knew of his dangerous situation would only precipitate the action before he was ready.

Moving easily, but carefully, to the fire, he glanced at the rifle propped against the tree, and he debated on making a dive for it. Reluctantly, he abandoned the idea. Instead, he scooped up the coffee pot and walked toward the stream as though to refill it.

Chu'ta's cold eyes followed the movement and he decided to wait until Clint returned to the fire. He shifted slightly and parted the small bush in front of him, easing the barrel of the carbine into the opening. The entire campsite lay under the open sight of the rifle.

He saw that Clint was no longer filling the coffee pot. He was nowhere in sight, and Chu'ta felt his flesh grow cold. Something had given their presence away and, without malice, Chu'ta cursed Cole for being a clumsy fool. The Apache never suspected that he himself had warned Clint of the trap.

A quick leap across the small stream and a silent plunge into the brush momentarily gave Clint a margin of safety, but he had no illusions about his chances in the woods armed with only a pistol.

He eased through the brush like a formless shadow. Clint knew that whoever was watching the campsite was bound to be armed with a rifle, and would now be doubly alert. He knew that his only chance was to get close enough to make sure of a kill with the handgun. Anything over twenty yards would be fatal to him, and he knew it.

Working carefully along the creek bank, Clint froze into stillness when he saw a dusty shadow filter through the brush on the other side of the stream toward the campsite. For an instant, the shadow froze, almost as though sensing Clint's presence. Then Chu'ta turned, and the harsh features of the Apache half-breed were momentarily clear in the shadows of the trees.

The long-barreled forty-four Remington was already in Clint's hand, his thumb cocking back the hammer. Chu'ta seemed to melt into the ground as the barking roar of the forty-four broke the stillness of the clear mountain air. A movement to the right was immediately followed by a second blasting roar from the smoking forty-four, and, in the space of heartbeats, Clint saw the Apache's body crush a bush under his falling weight, then lay still. Clint stood immobile, his gray eyes riveted on the body of the half-breed, not trusting the stillness of the Indian for a second. He knew that the only time you could figure an Apache was dead was when you saw his brains splattered on the ground.

Clint cautiously approached the half-breed, wading the small stream. He held the forty-four poised and ready to fire in his hand. He saw that Chu'ta was sprawled spread-eagled on his back, his sightless eyes staring at the sky. The brown face was as impassive in death as it had been in life. A gaping hole at the left center of the broad chest showed that death had been instantaneous. Another jagged bullet wound was higher up in his right shoulder, marking the first shot. Clint thought that it wasn't bad shooting against an Apache who had seen him.

He stood glancing around at the woods as he shucked the empty cartridges from the forty-four, punching fresh loads into the cylinders. Then, holstering the pistol, he reached down and lifted the carbine from the Apache's lifeless fingers. After propping it against a tree, he searched the body.

A leather pouch, heavy with new gold coins, was behind the half-breed's belt. Clint squatted by the body and counted the golden stream of double-eagles. Five hundred dollars. The price of a man's life in Pine Creek, Clint thought with anger.

Cole Neyland had taken a commanding position overlooking the whole camp. He had seen Clint return to the fire and scoop up the coffee pot, but his actions appeared unhurried and natural, so Cole didn't shoot. He wanted to give Chu'ta a chance to get into position, and there was no hurry.

Cole was a careful man who didn't believe in trusting to chance. He wasn't an especially good shot with a rifle to begin with, and the range was over a hundred yards; all downhill. He wanted Clint immobile; preferably sitting or laying down in case he needed a second or third shot.

Cole had been totally unprepared when he saw Clint leap across the stream and dive into the brush on the other side. Try as he might, he couldn't detect any movement, and he wondered how Jackson had discovered the ambush. It was inconceivable that Chu'ta had tipped his hand.

He waited anxiously for several long minutes, then he heard the muffled shots from the opposite side of the camp. Two dull explosions. Cole categorized the shots immediately as pistol shots, not the sharp crack of a rifle. He waited for several more minutes, straining his ears for further sounds, but none were forthcoming.

After a few minutes, Cole became worried, thinking that if Clint had gotten Chu'ta, then he, himself, was as good as dead.

Instantly making up his mind, Cole rose from the ground and noisily made his way back to his horse and mounted. He reined the steel-dust roan toward the wagon road as he circled Jackson's campsite in a wide arc. Then he eased the horse over the lip of the embankment of the road, and slid down a dozen yards to the roadway. Cole sank spurs deeply into the roan and beat a hasty retreat back to Pine Creek.

He told himself that he would meet with Jackson on grounds of his own choosing, and with weapons more suited to his deadly trade: six-guns at ten paces. It had been a mistake to follow the Texan into the woods, and Chu'ta had paid for the mistake with his life.

Cole felt no remorse for the dead Indian, because he knew that men who lived by the gun died by the gun. Nobody plying the deadly trade of weapons could look forward to another sunrise with any kind of assurance. There was always someone deadlier or faster, but, so far, Cole had yet to meet his match with a six-gun.

Clint hefted the sack of gold coins and stuck it behind his own belt. Then following the Apache's trail, he found the spotted mustang concealed in a nearby clearing. Following the trail back up the side of the hill, he discovered the other tracks beside the stream.

He saw that there had been two of them, and the other man was still unaccounted for. Hefting Chu'ta's carbine, he followed the other set of tracks into the woods, and read the story that they told him. The other man, a seeming tenderfoot in the woods, had hidden his horse and waited on the opposite side of the camp. Then he had left, moving fast. Clint managed a wry smile, but he realized how close a call he had had. If the roan hadn't tipped him off, he would have quickly become coyote and buzzard bait.

It didn't take much thought to figure out that the other bushwhacker had been Cole Neyland. The knowledge only hardened Clint's resolve to take care of Neyland—permanently. As Clint suspected, Cole gave no consideration to the code of the gunfighter, which advocated an even break in a stand-up, draw, and shoot. When he met the gunman there would be no question of giving him any sort of an edge. Cole Neyland was so fast he didn't need an edge anyway.

There remained the problem of what to do with the dead Indian. Thinking about that, Clint's eyes narrowed to a glittering hardness. Now would be as good a time as any to confront Silk Barrister, and put an end to this business in Pine Creek in a man to man way, that is, if the slimy snake had the stomach for it.

Clint retraced his steps and returned to the spot where he had gunned down Chu'ta. He then loaded the Indian on the spotted mustang. A few minutes later, Clint broke camp.

After throwing the saddle on the roan, he tied on his saddle bags and grub sack, and mounted. Leading the nervous mustang with its gruesome burden, he started down the wagon road for town; the forty-four Remington a reassuring weight on his hip.

CHAPTER TEN

Cole Neyland reined in his horse behind the loading dock of the trading post and hastily dismounted. Without knocking, he burst into the rear office, slamming the door behind him.

Silk Barrister looked up in surprise, noting the gunman's disheveled appearance; the string tie was slightly askew and the once brilliantly polished boots were scuffed and dirty. He raised his eyebrows inquiringly as the gunman approached the desk.

'Trouble, Silk,' Cole said in a rush. 'Jackson got Chu'ta in the woods southeast of town.'

'What happened?' Silk asked.

'We trailed Jackson north of town to where he made a circle, then we found his camp near a ridge overlooking the mines. Chu'ta circled the camp so we could catch him between us, but he caught onto the play somehow.'

'You mean that Clint Jackson took out Chu'ta and you failed to get him; is that it?' Silk asked, his voice filled with scorn.

Cole flushed and his jaw tightened in anger, while his cold gray eyes turned hard and glassy. 'I was out of my element and decided to withdraw. I will get Clint Jackson, but it will be with these,' he said, his hands resting on the butts of the holstered pistols on his hips. 'I didn't like the idea of going into the woods after him to start with.'

'Cole, I don't give a damn how you do it. I want Jackson dead. He has interfered with my plans for the last time. Are you

170

sure that he got Chu'ta?' Silk asked.

'I saw Jackson disappear into the woods,' Cole replied. 'Then, a few minutes later, I heard two pistol shots. Chu'ta had a pistol, but he was carrying that carbine of his. After the shooting, nobody came out of the woods.'

'Chu'ta might have gotten Jackson then,' Silk said quietly.

'No way,' Cole answered with certainty.

'This Clint Jackson must be a pretty tough character,' Silk replied thoughtfully. 'That's all the more reason to plant him on boot hill before he does even more damage to my plans.'

'Silk, I believe that I now know why he is in Pine Creek,' Cole said with satisfaction.

Silk Barrister raised his eyebrows and looked at Cole with increased interest as he asked: 'Why?'

'I think Shirley Claymore hired him,' Cole replied. He explained, 'When Chu'ta and I arrived at his campsite, her and Jackson were having a meeting, and were acting mighty friendly.'

'Shirley Claymore? Why would she hire a gunfighter and have him help Jeff Pickens?' Silk asked thoughtfully.

Cole curled his upper lips in a sneer, and

said: 'It's only an assumption, Silk, but this is the way I see it. She knows how Will Claymore feels about gunmen and taking the law into his own hands. So, if he found out that she hired Jackson to save his hide, then he would be mad as a grizzly. This way, she can move against you without it coming back on the Claymores, and without her husband finding out about it.'

He thought about it for a minute, then replied thoughtfully, 'Yes, Cole, it makes sense. Just this morning the bitch smiled boldly at me, and all the time she was planning to buy my beef. That's something to think about.'

But if the woman's craftiness galled Silk, it also brought forth a deep admiration for her. He had always thought the female was the more devious and dangerous of the species, and this only confirmed his belief. Still, man or woman, he wouldn't allow his plans to be interfered with, and he had to decide what to do about this new development.

Looking at Cole, Silk said quietly: 'I have got a little job for you to do before you take care of Clint Jackson.'

'Before?' Cole asked, wondering what Silk was planning now.

'Yes, I want you to escort Mrs. Claymore to a place of concealment, then hold her for a while. With her in my hands, Will Claymore might be willing to listen to my generous offers for the Fancy Nance,' Silk said with a flicker of a smile.

Cole took a minute to consider this new turn of events. For one thing, kidnapping a respectably married woman in the west was an extremely hazardous business. Nothing so angered the western male than having a woman abused, and it could lead to a necktie party very quickly.

He didn't have any scruples against it personally. In fact, his heartbeat quickened at the thought of having the uppity blonde beauty to himself for a while. But he knew that if he did this job for Silk, then it would be the last job he would be able to do in Pine Creek. Things would be too hot after that and he would have to clear out of the country. So he hesitated and said nothing for several minutes.

'What's the matter, Cole?' Silk asked evenly. 'Don't you have the stomach for the job?'

Silk had his own plans. He saw the danger of the situation as clearly as Neyland did, but he thought that Will

173

Claymore would make a quick deal to get his wife returned safely, and no finger would point at him if the deal was handled just right. Cole Neyland would be the scapegoat, of course, and a dead scapegoat could tell no tales. Silk figured that getting his hands on the Fancy Nance mine would be worth a few risks.

'It makes no difference to me how you want to handle things, Silk,' he replied evenly. 'If you want the woman, then you will have her.'

'All right, take her to the trapper's cabin on east butte. I'll have two of the boys bring up a load of supplies and move in. You know where the cabin is, don't you?' Silk asked.

'Yes.'

'Fine. The next time I see you, I want Shirley Claymore in my hands. Then you can take care of Clint Jackson.'

'Mrs. Claymore's price is a thousand dollars; payment in advance,' Cole said quietly.

'Make sure that I get my money's worth,' Silk said warningly.

'You will get it, Silk,' he replied, and watched Silk open the strong box and withdraw a roll of gold coins, then toss it to him.

Cole broke the seal on the roll of coins and poured them into his leather pouch, then left the office by the rear door. A minute later, he mounted the weary horse and rode down the alley to handle the chore for Silk.

Privately, Neyland thought Silk was a damn fool for the scheme, but it wasn't any of his business. It gave him a chance to get to know the uppity blonde before he took off for the Mexican border. When he was finished with her, Will Claymore wouldn't be wanting the damaged goods back.

He knew it was time to pull up stakes anyway, and he already had several thousand dollars in his moneybelt and more salted away in banks. He had enough to start a sizable spread south of the border and retire; fixed for life.

It was a smart man who knew when to get out of a dangerous business, and he had long been planning his retirement. Never a greedy man, he only wanted to be assured of comfort. He knew that people like Silk Barrister were never satisfied. They always wanted more and more, and accumulated money and possessions just for the sake of it as they got caught up in the vicious, never-ending circle of greed.

Coming to the end of the alley, Cole pulled up his horse as Clint Jackson rode by on his roan, leading Chu'ta's spotted mustang by the reins with the half-breed draped across the horse's back. Cole watched Clint's broad back as he proceeded down the street, but restrained himself from a back shot in town. It was broad daylight, and there were too many people on the street as witnesses.

Turning his horse, Cole rode back down the alley, then turned south to pick up the wagon road to the Claymore ranch. As he rode, he tried to visualize the ranch as he had seen it on several occasions. He thought that he might have to lay in wait in the timber until Shirley was alone and unprotected. But that was no problem, as he always had a bedroll tied behind the saddle, and the saddle bags held several days rations for emergencies. Cole was always prepared.

Within an hour, he arrived at the mountain meadow of the Claymore ranch and made camp high up in the timberline of the nearby slope. From there, he had a commanding view of the ranch house and outbuildings below. After he settled himself as comfortably as possible, Cole studied the movements below to get a pattern of how the ranch was run.

The ranch was a two-story affair with a high, peaked roof. Most houses and buildings in the high country had peaked roofs because of the heavy snowfall. The house had a double veranda. One on the bottom floor ran across the front and along both sides, and the other ran along both sides and across the back of the house on the second floor. A wide stairway led up to the second floor from the rear.

The house was surrounded on three sides by the outbuildings that were set well away from the main house. Cole saw a cook come out of the cookhouse and throw a bucket of water in the yard, scattering the hens that were pecking in the dirt. It was the most peaceful domestic scene that Cole had ever seen.

*   *   *

The forty-four Remington rested heavily, but comfortably, on Clint's thigh when he rode into Pine Creek with the half-breed tied over the saddle of the mustang. As he drew near Barrister's trading post, he checked to see that the gun was free of the hammer thong and the holster wasn't bound up.

Clint saw several idlers standing on the wide porch in front of the store, but two of them caught his special attention. They were obviously gunslicks, and were alike as two peas in a pod. They were the same size—both medium build, with long arms and sloping shoulders—and were equally armed with crossed six guns on their hips. Clint recognized them as the Clayton brothers, although he had no idea which one was which.

The Clayton brothers became alert at the same time and gave each other significant glances when they recognized Chu'ta's spotted mustang and the moccasins sticking out from under the folds of the blanket-draped body. They separated slightly, an unspoken understanding passing between them, and they were ready for action. Clint had seen the same play too many times before to mistake its meaning.

Several miners had stopped on the street and were watching the scene with a morbid interest. Everybody had recognized the Apache's horse and the burden that it carried. Some of them had heard the story of the hard-eyed cowboy on the roan. All of the men expected to see more trouble, and thought maybe there would be a gunfight between the cowboy and the two Clayton brothers, who were geared for trouble, as usual. A hush fell along the street and words were hurriedly passed into the gambling and drinking tents, bringing forth dozens of men to watch the anticipated action.

Clint reined the roan to a stop, facing the front of Barrister's Trading Post. He sat silent for a moment as he looked at the two gunslicks, noting their readiness and the hard looks in their pale blue eyes.

'Would one of you gents mind callin' out Silk Barrister,' Clint said in a low voice that carried up and down the street. 'I've got a little somethin' here that belongs to him.'

'Well now, cowboy,' Pete Clayton said in a slow southern drawl as he stood with his thumbs hooked in the crossed gunbelts. 'I might mind doing a lot of things. I usually don't handle Mr. Barrister's petty business for him.'

'You must be one of the Clayton brothers,' Clint said softly, his right hand resting on his thigh close to the forty-four.

He sat still in the saddle and didn't like

the position he was in, but knew it would be suicide to try and dismount under the eyes of the brothers. He realized that he had to take his chances from the back of the roan, who, thankfully was gun-trained not to buck or move around when the lead was flying.

'That's right, cowboy,' Pete replied with a sneer. 'I'm Pete, and this here is my brother, Tom.'

'I figured as much,' Clint replied coldly. 'You both look like a couple of yellow-bellied polecats.'

It took a moment for the words to sink in, and both of the brothers' faces registered astonishment. Things usually didn't go quite this way because a lone man knew when he was boxed and facing two relentless guns. The brothers reacted almost in unison, and both went for their guns simultaneously.

Pete Clayton went into a slight crouch as he reached for his guns, but Tom appeared to straighten as he began to pull at the twin pistols.

Pete was a shade faster than Tom, but he wasn't near fast enough. His right-hand gun had just cleared leather when Clint's first bullet caught him high in the chest, lifting him up on tiptoes as the impact of the heavy forty-four slug slammed him backward into the log wall of the store. Then his gun exploded harmlessly into the plank floor of the porch.

Tom Clayton cleared leather and fired a snap shot from the hip just as Clint turned the Remington in his direction. Clint felt the sharp bite and pull of the bullet when it hit him high and just behind his left shoulder, but it wasn't the numbing shock of a heavy hit, so he stayed in the saddle.

Time seemed to be suddenly suspended—the motion of Tom's thumb cocking back the hammer for another shot and the left-hand gun finally clearing leather—it all appeared as though it was happening in slow motion. Clint's own gun was already cocked and centered on the blond-haired gunman's chest, then the heavy forty-four bucked and roared in his hand as it belched a foot of flame and smoke from the barrel. Shock came into Tom's blue eyes as the heavy slug caught him high in the right shoulder, numbing his whole arm and spinning him around. The Colt revolver dropped from the suddenly dead and lifeless fingers. The second bullet caught Tom in the side of the neck and sent him skidding across the rough planks of the porch. He was dead before he hit the porch and came to rest in a grotesque heap.

Instantly turning his cold gray eyes and the deadly forty-four back on Pete, Clint saw that the other brother was lying against the log wall. He made a mighty effort to raise his six-gun for one last shot, but the task proved to be impossible. Pete's pale blue eyes suddenly glazed over and, with a final sigh, his head rolled to the side; dead.

Clint swept the bunch of men standing on the porch with his eyes and gun, but no one appeared to want any part of the gunfight that had just taken place before their eyes in the span of a few heartbeats. There wasn't a man on the street who wasn't stunned by what had just happened, and each man looked at Clint with various degrees of fear and respect.

Satisfied that no further trouble was forthcoming, Clint shucked out the empty cartridges and shoved in fresh loads. He saw a face appear in the window of the store, then saw a rounded figure come hurrying out of the back room toward the front of the building. Clint recognized McSweeny and figured that the approaching man was Silk Barrister.

Upon seeing Silk in the store, Clint called in a loud voice: 'Barrister! Silk Barrister!'

A minute later, Silk stepped through the doorway of the store and surveyed the scene with calm, appraising eyes, his thumbs hooked in his waist belt. He had paused to remove his coat, so there would be no question about him being unarmed.

Silk looked first at the two Clayton brothers, then at the spotted mustang with its gruesome burden. Finally he looked directly at the tall cowboy sitting quietly on the big roan. Silk's heart turned cold with fury as he glared at Clint sitting so calmly and assured. The man that was wrecking his plans and schemes was before him, and Silk was suddenly determined that no matter what the cost, Clint Jackson would die. If looks could kill, then Clint would have died on the spot.

'Barrister, my handle's Clint Jackson, and I don't take it kindly havin' hired killers sicced on me,' he said in a low, ominous tone.

Reaching in his belt, he took out the sack of gold coins that he'd found on Chu'ta's body. Then, with a contemptuous gesture, he tossed the pouch of gold at Barrister's feet.

'Barrister, I figure I'm worth more'n the five hundred you paid the half-breed,' he said coldly. 'Next time, mister, you'd better make it worth a man's while, 'cause if'n they don't get the job done, there ain't goin' to be a rock big enough for you to hide under. You get my meanin', Barrister?'

Silk made no reply. He just stood and glared at the soft-spoken cowboy, a deep hatred lighting up his dark eyes.

'Barrister, I surely wish you were wearin' a gun, but since you ain't, you'll live this time. If'n another attempt is made against me or the Sweet Lady, or Jeff Pickens, I ain't goin' to care if'n you're armed or not. I'll kill you on sight like I would a rabid dog, and think I'm riddin' the world of a slimy snake. I don't cotton to dry-gulchers and hired killers. You're a lowdown polecat of the worse kind, and not much of a man either. Barrister, you remember my warnin', 'cause you won't hear another one.'

With those words hanging in the tense air, Clint dropped the reins of the mustang. He reined the roan around, and rode slowly up the street toward the stable. He felt a dull throbbing in the back of his shoulder where the bullet had hit him, and it sent waves of pain coursing through his body.

He rode the roan directly inside the stable through the open doors, and wearily swung off the saddle. Mark Tollett was standing by when he dismounted, and the old man's clear eyes were crinkling with satisfaction.

'Youngster, you may not be a gunfighter, but you'll do 'til one comes alon'. Yep, you sure 'nuff wrecked old Silk's plans today, and cut his crew of skunks down to size,' he said evenly with a dry chuckle.

Mary McDonald stood off to one side. Her pretty face was white and strained looking, and the blood running down Clint's shirt wasn't going unnoticed. She quickly slipped past Mark and reached out tentatively to touch Clint's left arm.

'You're hurt,' she said reproachfully. 'Come into the office and let me look at that.'

Clint looked at Mary's earnest, worried face. He saw the freckles making a pretty pattern across her pert little nose and cheeks, and didn't argue. He followed her wearily to the tackroom. Just as they reached the door of the room, Kevin came skidding through the big barn doors, his young face flushed with excitement.

'Mary!' Kevin shouted breathlessly. 'You should have seen it!' Upon seeing Clint standing there, his face lit up and he hurried over to him. 'Gosh, you was quick. Quick as lightning. I never saw anything like it . . .'

'Kevin!' Mary snapped in quiet anger, stopping his breathless flow of words.

The boy looked slightly abashed for a moment. 'But he did, Mary. Didn't you, Clint?' He asked, turning worshipping eyes to the big man who was leaning gently on Mary's shoulder.

'That's right, partner,' Clint replied quietly. 'But right now, I need some tendin' to and a cup of hot coffee for sure.'

'Got the coffee,' Mark injected, 'and maybe a little somethin' extra to give it some flavorin'.'

'I can use it,' Clint replied, and they all entered the office. Clint added, 'Partner, will you see 'bout my horse?'

Kevin immediately left the room and Clint sank into one of the chairs. Mary quickly became busy with the buttons on his shirt.

'Missy, I can do that,' he said softly. 'Never had no girl undress me a'fore.'

'There's a first time for everything, mister, and I'm not a girl,' she said saucily as she kept at her self-appointed task until the shirt was off, revealing the jagged gash that ran across the shoulder going upward, almost to the back of the collar line.

'It ain't bad, youngster,' Mark observed professionally. 'Won't even need but a stitch or two, unless you want a scar.'

'I'll pass on the needle work, Mark. They're more trouble than a scar is,' Clint replied.

'Spoken like a real man,' Mary said bitingly, her blue eyes flashing. 'Afraid of a little needle. Humph!' She scoffed and flounced away to put a kettle of water on the stove. 'Mr. Tollett, will you get me some carbolic and clean rags,' she asked, and Mark went to his medicine chest in the stable to get the items needed to clean and dress the wound.

Mark chuckled at Mary's suddenly womanly manner, but Clint looked at her suspiciously. Within half an hour, the wound on Clint's back was cleaned and dressed, and he was fortified with a strong cup of whisky-doused coffee. Then he stretched out on Tollett's bed.

He quickly fell into a heavy sleep, unaware of the moves underway to make sure that his sleep went uninterrupted. Tollett cradled his shotgun under his arm, and took a seat just inside the stable doors, while Kevin got his father's thirty-six caliber Navy Colt, tucked it in his waist band, then sat near Mark.

Mary stayed by the bed and carefully studied the clean shaven features of the man who had captured her heart. Not that it made any difference, but she was relieved to see that he had masculine, rugged good looks which could be considered handsome.

His large work-scarred hand lay on the top of the blanket, and she took it in her small hands. Clint stirred slightly, but made no move to pull back his hand. His breathing was slow and regular, and his rugged features were relaxed.

If Clint had known what was going through Mary's mind, he would have saddled the roan and lit out for distant country. But he slept peacefully and unknowingly as she continued to hold his hand and fall evermore deeply in love with him.

Mary sat quietly by the bed for several hours until Mark entered the room and took in the scene with a shrewd sweep of his clear eyes. Then he prudently left without the cup of coffee he had come in to get. As Mark went back to his chair by the stable doors, he chuckled to himself. He knew that Clint had gotten himself roped and hog-tied, and figured that the branding iron wasn't far away.

CHAPTER ELEVEN

After Clint rode away from the trading post, Silk Barrister stood on the porch in a silent rage. He watched Clint ride up the street and disappear into the livery stable.

He looked again at the three dead men and his jaw tightened in anger and frustration. Three first-class gunfighters, and not one of them was able to handle Clint Jackson.

Silk wanted to make a grand gesture by leaving the pouch of gold lying on the porch, but the gesture was beyond him. He reached down and picked up the pouch, holding it in his hand for a moment. He knew that any man other than Jackson would have pocketed the gold and said nothing about finding it.

A heavy-set, barrel-chested man dressed in coarse clothing approached Silk and stood impassively as though waiting for orders. He was Henry Barlow, the man who ramrodded the dozen or more toughs Silk employed to keep the miners in line.

Barlow's flattened nose, scarred brows, and dull, insensitive eyes showed his calling as a rough and tumble man. His black eyes, fastened on Silk in neutral anticipation, revealed nothing of the thoughts that lay behind them, if indeed he had any. Silk regarded his chief bully for a moment. Then he gave instructions in a quiet, controlled voice, betraying none of the boiling anger he felt inside.

'Henry, take care of these three, then find Bill Spearman and both of you report to me,' Silk ordered.

'Yes sir, Mr. Barrister,' Barlow replied, and beckoned to two rough-looking men who were standing nearby.

Silk turned and strode purposefully through the store to his office, passing the frightened-looking McSweeny without even a glance.

Closing the door behind him, he took a seat in the padded swivel chair and yanked open a side drawer of the desk. Neatly wrapped in a cartridge belt was a worn holster holding a heavy forty-four caliber Navy Colt that had polished walnut grips. Silk looked at the gun and holster for several minutes, then, with a dismissive gesture, he slammed the drawer shut again. 'No way,' he thought. 'If I put that gun on, Jackson will kill me on sight.'

Silk could handle a gun, as most of the western men could, but he had no illusions about himself being a gunslick. Either one of the Clayton brothers pulling their guns left-handed could have beaten Silk to the draw, so he knew that he would not stand a chance in a shoot-out with Jackson.

However, there was more than one way to skin a cat, and he thought of the specially made sleeve holster for his single-shot forty-one caliber Derringer that was lying in a trunk in his cabin. Silk thought it would be wiser to oil the Derringer and carry it from now on.

With just a little practice, the spring-loaded arm holster would serve him very well, and would drop the small pistol into his waiting palm for a quick, careful shot.

It had worked for him in the past on the river boats along the Mississippi River, and it would work on Jackson, who was a born westerner and unused to such treacherous methods.

A light rap sounded on the door. Silk called 'Come in,' and looked up to see McSweeny standing nervously in the doorway. 'Yes, McSweeny, what is it?'

'Bill Spearman and Henry Barlow are outside.'

'Good. Send them in.'

'Yes sir,' he replied, then disappeared from the doorway to be replaced a minute later by the two barroom toughs.

Bill Spearman was a medium-sized man of slight build and clear features. He was a complete contrast to the powerful-looking Henry Barlow, but was every bit as brutal and unfeeling as Barlow was.

Silk waved the two men to chairs against the wall several feet from the desk. The men dropped into the seats and waited for Silk to speak.

'Henry, how many men can you round up before tomorrow morning?' Silk asked quietly. 'I want to run that old fool, Jeff Pickens, out of the Sweet Lady mine, and I need a good crew.'

Henry Barlow looked uncomfortable for a minute. He was well aware of the situation at the mine, and the old man's reputation with the big Sharps rifle. Barlow realized that getting men to go up against the granite walls of the mine shack wouldn't be easy.

'Mr. Barrister, I can lay my hands on twenty pretty good men,' Henry replied. 'But, whether they would go up against that old man and his rifle is another question. He shot the fingers off Tangle-Eye George from over sixty yards away, and Tangle-Eye was behind the timber pile. The men ain't forgot that.'

Silk sneered faintly at the man's obvious discomfort. No fist and boot bully ever wanted to go against guns, but there just wasn't time to send for gunslicks to handle the chore.

'The old man isn't going to have time to be doing any shooting,' Silk said evenly. 'That is, not if this job is handled right.'

'Well, now, if you have a plan...' Henry replied, leaving the remark hanging in the air.

'Of course I've got a plan,' Silk said impatiently. 'Listen, round up all the men you can and arm them with rifles. Have a dozen of them get behind the timber pile to keep the old man busy, and have the others sneak up on the shack from above with sticks of dynamite. We'll blast the old coot out, or else, bury him in that fort of his. There's a big bonus for the man who puts the final bullet in him. A thousand dollars.'

Both of the men raised their eyebrows in surprise at the amount of the bonus, and knew it would certainly put some fighting spirit into the men.

'Mr. Barrister, what about the rest of the men?' Henry asked, and added: 'Old Jeff Pickens is a hell of a shot, so some of them are bound to get wounded.'

'Every man will get a hundred dollars for the job, and fifty more for a wound,' Silk said.

Barlow nodded. The money would certainly satisfy his crew, and make them eager to do a good job. Each man would want to collect the thousand dollars, that was for sure.

'Okay, Henry,' Silk said evenly, 'go to it. Draw all the weapons, dynamite and whatever else you need from McSweeny. Before noon tomorrow, I want to see the Sweet Lady mine occupied by our men.'

Barlow stood up, and Bill Spearman rose

also, thinking that he was going to be part of the action, but Silk stopped him.

'Sit down, Bill. I've got some other plans for you,' Silk informed him.

Spearman dropped back into the chair and watched as Barlow left the office and pulled the door closed behind him. Then he saw that Silk was regarding him as if trying to judge him.

Speaking softly, Silk said: 'Bill, you once told me that there wasn't a job you wouldn't take on if the price was right.'

'That's right, boss,' he agreed. 'What have you got in mind for me to do?'

'How would you feel about holding a woman for me for a few days?'

'Hold her, or kill her?' Spearman asked in an even, neutral voice.

'Just hold her in an out of the way place until certain terms are met,' Silk answered.

Spearman thought over the proposition rapidly. It was dangerous to mess with women in the west. If he took on the job and she later pointed her finger at him, there would surely be a noose under a tree waiting for him. Releasing the woman meant he was finished in Pine Creek, and in Colorado. The price for the job would have to be high, more than just running money.

Maybe enough for a place of his own. A new start further west; California maybe.

'Boss, if the price is right, then I'm game for anything,' he replied firmly.

'A thousand dollars,' Silk said, and saw a light come in Spearman's eyes. 'You will have to pick out one other man to help you. One that's dumb and follows orders without question. He will get five hundred, and when the job is finished, it could be your bonus, if you follow what I mean.'

Spearman grinned, having understood Silk very well, and said: 'I'm game, boss. What's the plan?'

'Take a few days' grub for several people up to the old trapper's cabin on east butte. Cole Neyland will deliver a lady for you to watch, and you will take your orders from him. When Will Claymore signs over the Fancy Nance mine to me, then you will release her and clear out. Things will be too hot for you around here, and I wouldn't like it if you implicated me in the venture. Do I make myself very clear?' Silk asked evenly.

'Perfectly, boss,' he answered. 'I had a hankering for far country anyway.'

'Good,' Silk replied. Taking the cash box from the desk, he counted out five hundred in coin and put a thousand dollar roll of double-eagles with it. Handing it all to Bill, he said warningly: 'Make sure of the man you take with you. Don't choose anyone with any intelligence or imagination.'

'I got just the man in mind, boss,' Spearman answered as he put the money in his pockets. 'Don't worry about a thing.'

Silk nodded and Spearman left the office, pulling the door shut behind himself. Silk Barrister turned back to the desk and lifted a quart bottle of whisky from a pigeon hole, then poured a generous measure into a heavy glass.

He didn't usually drink during the day, but this was a special occasion. Although he had suffered several losses since Clint Jackson's arrival, it had spurred him to move decisively against Jeff Pickens and Shirley Claymore. Silk could already feel the laurels of victory descending on him. It was a heady feeling. With the Sweet Lady and the Fancy Nance in his hands, along with his other mines, he would soon be a rich man, and, thus, beyond the law.

Soon after Cole Neyland kidnapped Shirley, Will Claymore would sign away his mine. It would then free Neyland to take care of that pesky Jackson character. Once

Jackson was out of the way, Cole would be taken care of before he could tie Silk to the kidnapping of Shirley. Silk chuckled to himself as the plans and schemes unfolded in his mind. With satisfaction, he raised the heavy glass in a silent toast to himself, then drank it in one gulp. He enjoyed the dull warmth as the liquor surged through his heightened senses.

Silk's stomach rumbled in protest at the whisky. Wearily, he got up to return to his cabin to prepare a meal. It was almost beyond belief that no decent eating place had been established in Pine Creek, and Silk wondered if he should look into the possibilities of setting up a place that would serve edible food. But he put the thought aside as not meriting his attention at the moment. Besides, it would compete with his own businesses, such as Joe's. Although Joe served slop unfit for man or beast, he did bring in a profit along with the drinking and gambling.

Passing through the front of the store, Silk paused momentarily to say to McSweeny: 'I'll be back after dinner.'

'Yes sir,' McSweeny replied, glad to see Silk leaving.

In a disreputable-looking, smelly dugout at the edge of town, Bert Turner sat on a filthy mattress and cleaned his Springfield rifle. On a low table lay a forty-one caliber revolver, and a half-full bottle of whisky. Bert's head was swathed in a white bandage that covered his cigar-burned ear. The whisky was helping to mask the throbbing pain he felt in his ear.

Bert's sense of balance had been affected slightly by the injury and it caused him to move in a disjointed manner as though he were drunk. But since that was his usual state anyway, it was something people were used to seeing and he was used to coping with. Around his middle under the wool, checked shirt, he was wrapped tightly in corsetlike bandages.

The doctor had forbidden Bert to get out of bed this soon, but he had shrugged off the doctor's advice. The reason he was up and cleaning the familiar weapons was evidenced by the conspicuously empty bed against the opposite wall of the dugout.

The bed had been occupied by Nails Kelly, Bert's partner for over five years. They had enjoyed a good relationship, and had made a good team in a series of robberies and murders. Over the years a genuine liking had grown between them, and now Bert figured he owed it to Nails to avenge his death.

One of Silk's men had already stopped by and told Bert of the gunfight in front of the trading post, and mentioned that Jackson was holed up in Tollett's stable.

In his younger days, Bert had done some trapping in the Northwest Territory, so he knew quite a bit about tracking. What he thought to do was to keep an eye on Tollett's place, then follow Jackson out of town and shoot him down from ambush. He didn't have a thought of giving the deadly gunfighter an even break, especially since he still seethed in anger over the beating he had taken and the death of his friend. Everyone agreed that Jackson was greased lightning with the big six-gun of his, and Bert wasn't going to let him have a chance to use it.

Once he was satisfied the weapons were in good working order and fully loaded, he stood up and steadied himself against the table and the wall. He slipped on his heavy coat and stuck the bottle of whisky in one of the coat pockets, then shoved the loaded revolver into his belt. Bert hefted the Springfield by the barrel and used the stock as a cane as he left the dugout.

He immediately went to Joe's and got a small sack of grub and another quart of whisky, then picked up his horse from the small string behind Joe's place. Saddling the roan and tying the sack of food behind the bedroll, he led the horse to where he could watch both doors of Tollett's livery stable.

Bert settled down to wait forever if needed, taking occasional sips of whisky to dull the pain in his head and stomach. His eyes were bright with furious hatred and anticipation of getting even with Clint Jackson.

CHAPTER TWELVE

It was mid-afternoon when Clint finally stirred and opened his eyes. He glanced toward the small stove in the room and saw Mary stirring something in a bubbling kettle. That was what had awakened him; the appetizing smell of stew. His belly rumbled in anticipation of some good food.

'Missy, is it ready yet?' Clint asked. 'I'm hungry enough to eat a horse.'

She glanced at him, a smile crossing her pretty face, and said softly: 'There's more than enough and you're up in plenty of time for a share of it.'

Clint threw off the blanket and sat on the edge of the bed. He moved carefully because of the tightness in his shoulder and back. The wound had begun to crust and the bandage was already stuck firmly to the torn flesh.

He looked around for his shirt and felt as uncomfortable under Mary's watchful eyes as he had when Shirley had found him in the pool that morning. Not seeing any sign of his shirt, he pulled on his boots instead, then looked for his hat and put it on. Rising gingerly, he stomped into the boots and looked around for his gunbelt, feeling more naked without it than without the shirt.

'It's on the table,' Mary said scornfully, and pointedly turned her back on him.

Clint crossed to the table and buckled on the gunbelt, then adjusted it about his waist and tied the bottom of it to his leg. As he checked to make sure the forty-four was loaded, he saw a shirt lying on the table, but saw it wasn't his own.

'You can wear that shirt until I can sew and wash yours,' Mary informed him pertly from the stove. 'It was my pa's, and you are about the same size.'

'Much obliged, missy,' he said gratefully, and slipped gingerly into the clean shirt, buttoning it up and tucking it into his belt.

Tollett came into the room carrying a shotgun and smiling. 'Glad to see you up and 'round,' he said sincerely.

'He should have stayed in bed,' Mary said defensively, knowing that you could sooner cage the wind than keep a vital man in bed. 'It's much too soon for him to be up and maybe getting himself shot again.'

'Missy, I'm not partial to gettin' shot at,' Clint said softly with a smile. 'Right now, I'm more interested in wrappin' my tongue 'round some of that tasty smellin' stew you're fixin' there.'

'Youngster, you won't be disappointed,' Mark said. 'She's the best little cook in Colorado.'

Mary blushed prettily under the praise and turned her head away in modesty, then said demurely: 'Get some plates and stop your blarney. It's enough to turn the head of any woman the way you have been

203

carrying on about my cooking.'

The two men complied promptly, and soon had savory plates of thick stew in front of them, along with thick slices of cornbread. The Irish stew was thick with chunks of beef, potatoes, carrots, onions, and broth.

After a few minutes, Tollett sat back contentedly and loosened his belt, then sipped his coffee as he watched Mary and Kevin eating. Looking at Clint, he asked quietly: 'Youngster, what're you plannin' to do now?'

'Well, Mark, I'm goin' out to talk to Will Claymore,' he replied, and pushed the empty plate away. 'I met Shirley Claymore this mornin' just before Chu'ta jumped me and we had quite a talk. I think if'n this trouble's goin' to be cleared up once and for all, then everyone should lend a hand. I'm goin' to give the Claymores a chance to join the fun.'

'Fun!' Mary snapped angrily, standing with her small fists balled up on her hips as she glared at Clint. 'A lot of fun it'll be when some coward shoots you down from behind.'

Clint looked at the girl with amusement and a light sparkle showed in his gray eyes as he said: 'Well, missy, I'll just have to see it don't happen.'

'Humph,' she sniffed, turning away indignantly.

'Youngster, I hate to throw a cold towel over your plans, but Will Claymore ain't goin' to go alon' with a vigilante party,' Mark said evenly. 'His brother, Paul, might, but he ain't got the influence to get the others to go alon' with him. They're all waitin' for Will to say "that's 'nuff" and lead 'em in the fight.'

'Maybe I can stoke his fire a little,' Clint said. 'Every man has a point to reach, so when Will says "that's 'nuff," then maybe he's reached his.'

'Don't count on it,' Mark replied pessimistically.

'Okay, I won't,' Clint said. 'But I'm countin' on you.'

Tollett looked at him keenly and asked: 'How so, youngster?'

'Mark, I'm kind'a worried 'bout Uncle Jeff bein' up at the Sweet Lady all by himself. I'd sure feel a mite better if'n he had a little help up there. Could you take a few days to sort'a help him out at the mine?'

'Been wantin' to do it for quite a spell,

but had to stay here to run the supplies up to the mine and take care of the stable,' Mark said. 'Of course, old Jeff might not take to the idea, but I think he'll let me stay once I get there.'

'Well, I'll count on that then,' Clint said, and asked: 'Can you get someone in to handle the stable while you're gone?'

'Got a part-time man now. One of the miners who got hurt a while back. If'n Kevin will agree to help him, then things should be all right for a few days.'

'How 'bout it, missy?' Clint asked. 'You mind if Kevin helps out 'round the place for a while?'

'Of course not,' she replied promptly. 'I'll even help myself.'

'Good, then I won't have to worry 'bout draggin' you outta any more saloons,' Clint said, and winked at Tollett.

'Drag me out! Why ... of all the low-down, hammer-headed ... the gall of you, Clint Jackson!' Mary sputtered in flashing anger, her eyes searching for a suitable weapon to strike him with. 'I'll ... I'll ...'

But when she turned around with a large spoon in her hands, Clint was slipping through the door of the tackroom with Mark close behind, a smile upon his lips

206

and a merry chuckle coming from his throat.

Outside the room, both men guffawed loudly as they approached the stalled roan and began to saddle him.

'Hold on, youngster,' Mark said, taking the forty pound saddle from Clint. 'Let me do it 'fore you open up that scrape on your back.'

The roan was saddled and bridled when Kevin came up, the heavy Navy Colt visible in the waistband of his trousers.

'You leaving, Clint?' Kevin asked.

'Yep, got to take a little ride, partner,' Clint replied. 'How 'bout openin' the back doors and droppin' the corral fence for me so I won't have to dismount?'

'Sure,' Kevin replied, and ran to do Clint's bidding.

'Mark, what's that youngster doin' with the thumb-buster?' Clint asked evenly. 'He'll be lucky if'n that hogleg don't blow his foot off.'

'He was a-guardin' you, youngster,' Mark replied. 'Never seen a boy so heated up and serious 'bout doin' something'.'

'Well, if'n I get a little time, I'll have to teach him how to use it, I guess,' Clint said with a smile.

Clint mounted up and touched spurs to the roan as he headed for the back doors of the stable. Then he rode into the corral, keenly alert for any signs of an ambush or a stake-out man. As soon as he cleared the doorway, he slapped the roan with the reins and put him into a gallop, going through the back corral gate in a thunder of dust.

Kevin watched Clint disappear around a tent house, then into a narrow lane beyond. He replaced the rails of the gate and walked back into the stable where Mark was waiting for him.

At the outskirts of town, Clint pulled the roan into a slow canter and put him on the narrow road leading to the Claymores' mountain ranch. He rode with caution because the road would make a perfect place for an ambush. Without conscious thought, he noticed the tracks of three horses on the rocky road. Two riders and a pack horse from the looks of the sign. Somehow the tracks seemed out of place, and for no particular reason, Clint found himself following the tracks with his eyes whenever the road wasn't too rocky.

A couple of miles out of town the tracks turned off and followed an almost invisible trail up the side of the pass, and, without pausing, Clint turned the roan to follow them. Topping the rise a while later, he saw the trail wind down into a small, narrow valley that had a stream running through it. In a clearing, he saw a spiral of smoke rising from a log cabin that was nested under a grove of trees next to the stream.

Putting the roan on the downward trail, the scene was quickly lost from his sight by the trees and brush. At the bottom of the trail, Clint made a wide circle and crossed the stream well below the cabin and came out on the other side. He ground-hitched the roan in a dense tangle of trees and underbrush, then proceeded on foot to within fifty or sixty yards of the cabin where he concealed himself in a clump of brush.

He saw that there was a small corral behind the cabin and there were three horses in it. He also noticed two slicker-covered saddles on the top rail of the corral fence. Since there was no one outside the cabin, Clint took a minute to study the surrounding terrain.

Clint could see no sign of any mine shaft in the hillside, but lying on its side, next to the stream, was a broken rocker box, evidence of a few shafts that had sunk into the banks of the stream. Since there was no evidence of any recent mining activity, and no crop or cattle in sight, he wondered what the two men were doing in such an out-of-the-way spot.

Before long, a bearded man came out of the cabin and emptied a bucket of dirty water. Then he carried it to the stream to refill it.

The man was dressed like a miner—rough pants and shirt, shin-high, flat-heeled boots, and a miner's wool cap—but the pistol stuck in the waistband of his pants was completely out of place at the remote cabin.

After a few minutes, a second man came out of the cabin and stood looking into the hills. He was dressed the same as the first, but he was clean shaven and of medium build and height. He took a stogie from his shirt pocket and lit it with a long match. Then, as the other man returned from the stream, they said a few words and the bearded man went inside.

Having seen all that he needed to, Clint backed away and went to the roan. He began following another route, which he believed to be parallel to the wagon road. From the rise of the hill, he saw the ribbonlike cut of the road below him and headed the roan towards it. He continued his journey to the Claymore ranch, thinking about what he'd seen.

Clint was sure that he had seen the bearded man in the small crowd that had gathered at Barrister's trading post when he'd shot it out with the Clayton brothers. If that was the case, then Silk might have some kind of interest in the out-of-the-way cabin. Clint wondered just what it could be.

Meanwhile, Bert Turner was wondering at Clint's interest in the seldom-used trail leading to the cabin. Bert, who had followed Clint from Mark's stable, concealed himself just over the top of the ridge.

As far as Bert knew, this was the only trail in or out of the valley, and he quickly spotted a perfect place to set up an ambush. The place was concealed behind a nest of boulders just over the rise, and gave a perfect field of fire against anyone making the climb up the trail. Tying his horse in a clump of trees, he took out his rifle and a bottle of whisky, then settled down to wait.

After about an hour, a movement caught the corner of his eye. Bert turned just in time to see Clint top the rise of the valley almost a mile beyond and disappear from sight.

Throwing caution to the wind, Bert marked the spot that he'd seen Clint disappear, then got his horse and returned to the road. He rode hard to reach the place where Clint had come out of the valley, and, sometime later, he found what he was looking for: the tracks of Clint's horse were still heading along the wagon road.

Bert followed the tracks and saw where Clint turned off the main road onto a private trail leading to the Claymores' ranch. 'So, the cowboy has been hired by the Claymores,' Bert thought. That explained Clint's trouble-making presence in Pine Creek: sob-singing Will Claymore had hired himself a gunfighter.

Bert Turner sat for a minute and considered everything. Since Clint had come on the trail from town, he would most likely be returning the same way. That being the case, all Bert had to do was hole up and wait until Clint Jackson finished his visit with the Claymores. Bert reined his horse around and headed back down the road as he searched the hillside for the place he wanted.

Clint rode up to the ranch and drew rein before a pole gate across the trail. He dismounted and worked the wire latch. After he led the roan through, he shut and refastened the gate. In the distance, he could see the ranch house set on a slight rise of land surrounded by outbuildings and enclosed in a ring of tall trees. The meadow leading to the ranch buildings was heavily carpeted with lush grass that was hock-high on the roan and green with newness.

A sizable horse herd grazed nearby, and heads raised inquisitively at the sight of the newcomers. A rusty-red stallion galloped out challengingly to stand snorting and pawing the ground as he tossed his head in warning that this was his herd.

The stallion was fierce and proud. Broad-shouldered, long-legged, and smooth-lined. Muscles rippled in fluid grace beneath his coat, which reflected the rays of the sun with a deeply burnished, red-gold color. The thick neck of the stallion bowed, arched in challenge as his forefeet came down together with hard jarring crashes as he showed off his fine points to the intruders.

Clint watched the animal's antics in fascination, admiring the fine specimen of horse flesh. Then, touching spurs to the roan, he turned toward the ranch house and rode along in an easy trot. The stallion paced them from the side for several hundred yards, then, when he was satisfied that he had scared off the intruders, he returned to the herd with a final snort. His neck was arched, his head held proudly erect.

Approaching the house, Clint saw that a lot of work had gone into its construction. The house was large; two stories high with a peaked roof, and a wide veranda along the front and sides.

It was built of squared logs, notched and set tightly together, then chinked with moss and clay. Off to both sides of the house and set back a way were the outbuildings: cookhouse, bunkhouse, smokehouse, barns, and corrals. It was easy to see that Will Claymore had built the place to last and had been in possession of it for a long time.

Clint reined in at the hitch rail in front of the house and dismounted, then tied the roan to the post with a careless drop of the reins. The roan immediately began to chew on the rail as countless other horses had done before him.

A tall, well-built man of about fifty, with iron gray hair and even grayer eyes, stepped out the door and stood on the porch looking at Clint. He was dressed in dark suit pants, which were tucked into calf-high cowman's boots, and white shirt. He was hatless, but he wore a heavy six-gun belted around his waist. From the description given to him by Uncle Jeff and Mark Tollett, Clint recognized the man as Will Claymore, and nodded toward him in a friendly manner.

'Howdy,' Clint said. 'Am I right in supposin' that I'm talkin' to Will Claymore?'

The man immediately tensed up, taking special note of Clint's rugged appearance and the way he wore the heavy pistol tied low to his right thigh. It was not an encouraging sight, but Will Claymore, although a prudent man, didn't fear the devil himself, and doubted that Silk Barrister would have the nerve to have him killed on his own doorstep.

'You suppose right, mister,' he replied firmly. 'Now state your business.'

'Mr. Claymore, my handle's Clint Jackson. Jeff Pickens is my uncle. Earlier today, I talked with your wife and she suggested that I come out and talk to you 'bout our mutual interests in Pine Creek,' Clint said evenly.

'I've heard a lot about you since yesterday, Mr. Jackson,' Claymore said, relieved. 'News, especially good news, travels fast here in the mountains. Come in. I'd like to talk with you.'

Clint loosened the cinch strap on the roan, then mounted the four steps to the porch and entered the house as Claymore stood to one side and held the door open. Clint swept off his flat-crown hat and looked around at the entrance foyer, then hung the hat on one of the wall pegs, but didn't remove his gunbelt when he saw that Will continued to wear his own.

'Welcome to the Five-star ranch, Mr. Jackson,' he said, shaking hands. 'Come into the parlor and have a drink.'

'Much obliged, Mr. Claymore. Don't mind if'n I do,' Clint replied softly. 'If'n you don't mind, I'd rather you call me Clint. That "mister" part kind'a sticks in my ear. I'm just not used to titles like that.'

'All right, Clint, have a chair and call me

Will,' he said, waving to a leather chair as he walked over to a small cabinet and lifted a bottle and two glasses out of it. Carrying the glasses over to Clint's chair, he handed him one and filled it almost to the brim, then poured one for himself.

Setting the bottle on the table between them, he took a seat directly across from Clint, then raised his glass in a toast. 'To law and order,' Will proposed quietly.

'Can't argue with those sentiments,' Clint said, and drank off half of his drink. He enjoyed the smoothness of the Kentucky whisky, which was a pleasant change from the barroom bottles.

The parlor was a large, oblong room paneled in aged pine that was darkened with polish. At the far end of the room was a gray stone fireplace and a stone mantel above it. The fireplace almost covered the whole outside wall of the room. The skin of an enormous grizzly bear, with the head still intact and showing a fierce snarl, lay in front of the fireplace.

Along the inside wall was a fancy gun cabinet containing several dozen shotguns and rifles. All were cleaned and oiled, and gleamed dully in the light from the several lamps already lit and giving off a cherry glow. Everywhere on the walls trophy heads were mounted: deer, antelope, bighorn sheep, and bear.

The furniture was made of polished oak, heavy and masculine looking. There wasn't a dainty piece of furniture anywhere in the room. The chairs and couches were covered with dressed and tanned deerhide. Still, there were feminine touches about the room. The lamp bases had lace coverings. Finely crocheted pieces of cloth protected the brilliantly polished tables, and fancy pillows were scattered around on the couches and chairs.

Finished with his drink, Clint was about to set the empty glass on the small table when Claymore waved at the bottle setting between them and said: 'Help yourself, Clint. Don't be bashful.'

'Don't mind if'n I do,' he replied, pouring himself another stiff shot.

'Clint, I've heard of your run-ins with Barrister's hired men, and my wife told me about your talk earlier today,' Will said quietly. 'But I'd like to hear the whole story from start to finish, if you don't mind telling me.'

'No, Will, I don't mind at all,' Clint replied, then proceeded to give him a full account of everything that had transpired since his arrival in Pine Creek.

The older man sat forward several times during the narrative with a pleased smile on his face. During the talk, Shirley came into the room, and, after suitable greetings, she sat quietly by her husband and listened to Clint's story with as much interest as Will.

She was wearing a plain housedress, but it did nothing to hide her youthful beauty, perfection of form, and vitality within her. Her long blonde hair was down, but caught up in a net and held in a half-bun behind her head. Her hair caught glints from the lamp light and appeared like finely polished gold.

As Clint talked, he compared the Claymores. The heavy, rocklike and serious Will was twice his wife's age, but was still showing good health and strength. Shirley, light as a butterfly, a lovely goddess captured in human form, was voluntarily chained to a man old enough to be her father.

It took no great insight to know that it was Shirley who had done the capturing. Will had been a bachelor when he went east. The only women he had ever known were the kind found in saloons and brothels. But when a woman sets her sights on a man and is determined to have him, if the man doesn't have a fast horse and a head start, then he usually ends up hogtied and branded before he knows what's going on. However, if Will was hogtied and branded, he didn't seem to mind the strings, nor the brand. His eyes went soft when he looked at his young and beautiful wife, and, almost unconsciously, he tenderly covered her hand with his from time to time.

When the story ended, a silence hung in the air for several moments. Shirley broke it by jumping up, which caused the men to get slowly to their feet in courtesy, but she said with a smile, 'No, no, don't get up. I'm just going to get the cigar box so you men can talk and smoke.'

Then, crossing to the desk, she returned with a canister of mellow cigars. They each took one and leaned forward to light them from the match that Shirley struck and held. They both sat back contentedly while she poured them another drink. Then she took her seat beside Will, just touching him with her shoulder.

A while later, Clint finished outlining what needed to be done to get Barrister out of Pine Creek, and he felt dry as old shoe leather. He sipped his drink as Will pondered over what Clint had said.

'Clint, you have had a very busy time for so short of a stay in our territory, but you forget one thing. There is no proof that Silk Barrister is actually paying those men you had trouble with. There are always thugs and riffraff in every new town like Pine Creek, along with the gamblers, conmen, hustlers, and the women. A man is going to spend his wages, or gold, and nothing is going to change human nature,' Will said quietly.

'Will, nobody denies workin' for Silk Barrister, and it's his paid gunnies and bullies I've been talkin' 'bout and that I've had trouble with,' Clint replied evenly. 'I'm not talkin' 'bout runnin' the gamblers and girls outta town. Just Barrister and his crew of skunks. It's lon' past time for a noose to end their game and make it so decent folks can live and work in peace.'

'I fully agree with you,' Will said. 'But there isn't one shred of proof that Barrister is behind those men. Get me proof that Barrister is behind or connected with the disappearance of those miners, and we will rise against him and give him his dues.'

221

'Will, I don't see what additional proof you need. They've already taken shots at you and your brother. In plain sight of our mine you can see the men standin' guard over Uncle Jeff's mine. Frankly, I just don't understand your attitude,' Clint said evenly.

The older man looked uncomfortable for a moment. Then he began to speak in a slow, hesitant voice: 'Clint, a long time ago, I was with a vigilante posse looking for rustlers. We came on three men. One of them was just a youngster of about thirteen. We held a trial on the spot. The evidence looked condemning and a vote was taken to hang them. I admit that I also voted for the rope.'

Will paused for a moment and rubbed his big hands together, then continued slowly: 'All of them pleaded that they weren't guilty and the boy even cried, but we hardened our hearts against them and soon the deed was done. Everyone of us ranchers felt self-righteous and we didn't give the matter another thought until a month later when a U.S. marshal sent word that he had the rustlers in custody, and they had admitted their guilt in trying to lighten the sentence.'

He looked across at Clint with anguish stamped on his face, and said: 'You can imagine how I felt. I helped to hang three innocent men. But the evidence had been so strong that they were the ones who had done it. They were found right on the trail of the cattle and had new gold pieces in their saddlebags. I made a vow that I would never again participate in a vigilante posse, no matter how strong the evidence of guilt was. The guilty must be punished in a court of law; not with guns and ropes in the hands of vengeful men.'

Clint could understand how Will felt. The man was carrying a heavy burden of guilt. But now he'd gone to the opposite extreme, and that was just as bad. Maybe even worse, because it lent silent support to Barrister's activities and evil deeds.

'Will, there's no law in Pine Creek,' Clint stated flatly. 'When decent men gather in one spot to live together, there has to be some kind of law and order, or else the strong will push down the weak. Where there's no law, then a man must carry his law on his hip and use his best judgment as to what is right and what is wrong. It's as simple as that.'

'For you, maybe, but not me,' Will said

with a heavy sigh. 'Clint, I believe you're a capable and a decent man. What I can do is this: I can appoint you town marshal. Then you can deputize as many men as it takes to clean up Pine Creek once and for all.'

'Will, I'm not a lawman,' Clint protested. 'I just came to Pine Creek to help my uncle in a family matter. Once a man gets to wearin' a star, he's marked for life. I'm not anxious to get that brand on my hide.'

'Why don't you think it over before you turn it down?' Will said reasonably. 'Whether you realize it or not, you were born to wear a star, and it's only right that the best man accepts the responsibility. Many decent men who have worn a star have been gunned down in the streets because they lacked the ingredients you have in such abundance: fortitude and skill with weapons. If you think of all the weaker citizens as your family, then you will see that I know what I'm talking about.'

'I don't know,' Clint replied thoughtfully. 'I'll give it some thought.'

'Clint, you do that, and let me know. If you agree to wear a star, then I'll call an association meeting and we'll elect a judge and all the rest of the trappings of a real town, then back your play all the way. That's the best I can do for you under the circumstances.'

'I understand,' Clint said.

'Meantime, gentlemen,' Shirley injected, 'it's close to supper time and you must stay and eat with us, Clint.'

Will was quick to agree with his wife, and Clint gave over with good grace, since he was hungry anyway. They retired to the dining room as soon as the Mexican cook announced that supper was ready. There was plenty to eat: fresh beef, canned vegetables, freshly baked bread, and a fluffy chocolate cake to finish the meal off with. Clint did justice to the meal and was glad he'd stayed to eat with the Claymores.

CHAPTER THIRTEEN

About the time that Clint was sitting down to supper at the Claymores, Mark Tollett and Kevin McDonald were riding out to the Sweet Lady mine.

Mark carried his big .12 gauge double-barreled shotgun and several boxes of shells, and Kevin was along so he could return the horse to the stable after they reached the mine.

Dusk was rapidly approaching and the sun was a dull red ball hanging just over the western peaks of the Rockies, bathing the mountains in an aura of golden and purple haze.

'Mr. Tollett, why does my sister, Mary, act so funny when Clint's around? I've never seen her do such crazy things before, and him old enough to be our father,' Kevin said.

Mark chuckled for a moment, then replied: 'Boy, Clint ain't quite that old. Not more'n thirty, I'd say. Your sister has done set her cap for him sure 'nuff, and if'n she has her way, you're liable to end up with Clint as a brother-in-law.'

The thought of Clint as a brother, even an in-law one, caused Kevin's face to light up in joy. If that was Mary's game, then he would try to help her catch Clint, but one thing was certain: she would have to stop her bossiness, or Clint would take to the hills and she would never trap him. He decided to speak to her about it when he returned to the stables.

'That's great, Mr. Tollett,' Kevin said

cheerfully. 'I'd sure like Clint for a brother-in-law.'

'Yep, you just might see it, boy. Clint's reached the age, whether he knows it or not, when he's lookin' for a place to settle and someone to settle with. I think Mary would be the best thin' that ever happened to him, even if'n she is a mite young. But girls have been known to marry a whole lot younger'n she is.'

'I know,' Kevin said. 'Back home, Anabelle LeMay got married when she was fifteen. That's two years younger than Mary is. Mary's always saying that she's not going to be an old maid at eighteen, which she'll be in a few more months. Already she's using ma's perfume and even rubbing cream on her face at night to get rid of her freckles.'

'I think freckles are right cute,' Mark said, then added: 'Well, here we are, boy. I don't see no lookout watchin' the mine, do you?'

'No sir,' Kevin replied.

Both man and boy searched the surrounding rocks and gullies, but saw no sign of any of Silk Barrister's men. Mark dismounted and handed the reins of the horse to Kevin.

'Soon's I'm inside,' he said, lifting the shotgun from under the saddle fender, 'you skedaddle on back to the stables. Take care of my mules and horses, boy.'

'Yes sir.'

Mark nodded and began the climb up the rocky slope toward the mine shack. Swinging his gimp leg awkwardly over the rough ground, he stopped some thirty or forty yards below the shack and called out: 'Jeff! Jeff Pickens!'

After a silence of several moments, a voice from inside the shack answered: 'What in tarnation are you doin' here you old horny-toad?'

'Came to keep you company. It's gotten plumb lonesome in town since you've turned into a hermit, you old coot. Open up while it's still light 'nuff for me to see the ground without fallin' and breakin' my fool neck.'

'Well, come on in if'n you're such a dan' fool. Don't know if'n you'll ever be able to get back out,' Jeff called.

Mark turned and waved to Kevin, who turned the horses and headed back into town as Mark limped toward the shack. The door swung open and he limped inside, then looked around as Jeff barred

228

the door after him.

The place was considerably better stocked than on his last visit several months before. There were boxes, bags, and barrels lining the granite walls of the large shack, and a savory smell came from the rock stove and fireplace combination in the corner.

Moses eyed Mark suspiciously. Since the old man was known to him, he wasn't growling, but he wasn't friendly either. Seeing the two old-timers pumping hands in friendship, Moses gave a snort and retired to the large bone he kept in the corner and began to sharpen his teeth.

The two men sat at the table and looked at each other in the gruff way which marked true old-time friendship, yet masked their true affection for each other.

'What's that nephew of mine up to?' Jeff asked.

Mark leaned forward eagerly, glad of an excuse to tell of Clint's latest exploits at Barrister's trading post. Jeff hung onto every word, asking sharp questions to get every fact straight in his mind as the story unfolded with many embellishments and lucid details. Tollett's face showed satisfaction when the story was finished and

Jeff's face glowed with high excitement.

'Yep, that boy is a Jackson and a Pickens all right,' Jeff said with a merry chuckle. 'Took out both the Claytons at the same time. Who'd of thought it? What's he doin' now?'

'He went out to the Claymore ranch. Wants to talk Will and Paul into cleanin' out this nest of snakes. Of course, he's got 'bout as much chance of it happenin' as a snowball lastin' in the desert. Personally, I think Will is goin' to try and talk Clint into takin' the sheriff's badge. Do you think he will?'

Jeff gave the matter some serious thought, then he shook his head negatively, and said: 'Nope, wouldn't be natural. No Jackson or Pickens ever toted a star 'fore, and I don't look for the boy to be the first. Looks like the boy's got a lone hand to play. Only two thin' a-worryin' me right now is Cole Neyland or some dirty back-shooter. Boy's pretty sharp and can look out for his backtrail, but what 'bout Cole Neyland? The man's uncanny with a six-gun from everythin' I've heard 'bout him. Worse, the boy has seen him in action, and knows what he can do. That just might cut his confidence down some.'

'Jeff, from what I seen with my own eyes, the boy can hold his own with the best of 'em. He's so dan' fast, I didn't even see his pull, and he got Pete just as he cleared leather, and Tom 'fore he could thumb a second shot, or even pull his left-hand gun. The boy's like greased lightnin', Jeff. Never seen such a pull a'fore. If'n I didn't know better, I'd swear that he must'a had the gun in his hand already cocked when the fight began.'

Jeff's eyes flashed briefly in anger, but before he could speak in his nephew's defense, Mark held up his hand and said: 'Now Jeff, I didn't say he did. Just sayin' that he's so fast, you miss his draw. Never seen nothin' like it a'fore and don't expect to again; that's all.'

'Okay, thought you was castin' a slur,' Jeff said gruffly.

'No way, Jeff. Done got attached to that boy, sure have,' Mark said quietly.

'The youngster that rode up with you, is he Kevin McDonald?' Jeff asked.

'Yep. His sister, Mary, done set her cap for the boy, too. Right pretty little thin', she sure is,' Mark said with a chuckle.

'Might not be a bad idea,' Jeff replied with a grin. 'It's 'bout time the boy was a-thinkin' 'bout settlin' down. He's sure gonna be fixed up if'n we come outta this ruckus with our skins.'

'What're planning on doin', Jeff?' Mark asked, and added: 'That boy might be needin' somethin' 'cause it's already too late to head for the hills as far as the girl is concerned, it sure is,' Mark said, and chuckled dryly.

'I've thought 'bout it quite a bit. First off, all my kinfolks are goin' to get a share, especially Clint. Then I'm gonna take a long trip across the ocean and see all 'em sights that I've ever heard tell of. You ever want to visit Paree?' Jeff asked with a twinkle in his eyes.

'Yep, thought 'bout it a time or two,' Mark admitted, then grinned ruefully. 'Don't know as it would do any good now.'

'Well, when all this is over, we'll see 'bout it,' Jeff said.

'We?'

'Yep. You don't think I'm a-goin' to go traipsin' all over the world without my oldest and best friend, do ya? You're comin' with me a-course,' Jeff said positively.

'I don't know 'bout that, Jeff,' Mark replied. 'The idea might take some gettin' used to.'

'Think it over. I'd feel awful funny with all 'em furriners all by myself. 'Course we ain't outta this scrape yet, but now that Clint's here, I'm breathin' easier. Thought I had it all set, sittin' here behind these walls, but you know what that youngster said when I showed him my defenses?'

'No, what?'

'Well, I showed him my stout walls, hoard of ammunition and clear fields of fire. Told him how safe I was here in this shack, and he took one look 'round and said, "In fact, you're immobilized,"' Jeff chuckled and continued, 'Pretty smart youngster he is. He wouldn't hear of stayin' behind these walls and workin' the mine in shifts. Said he'd be the attack force rovin' 'round outside, hittin' the enemy where it hurts, like an Apache. Lord, the boy should have joined the Army. He is a natural for tactics and such like.'

'Well, Jeff, he's right,' Mark agreed. 'But you are too. You couldn't very well leave the mine unprotected, or Silk would have already been in here, linin' his pockets with your gold.'

'Yep, still it's a lucky chance that brought the boy here right when I needed him the most,' Jeff said, eying Mark suspiciously when he suddenly seemed embarrassed and couldn't meet his eyes. 'You! You old horny-toad! You sent for him, didn't you?' Jeff asked, knowing the truth without an answer.

Mark swallowed noisily and shifted his eyes around the shack as he tried to think of what to say. He always found it hard to tell a lie, especially to a friend. But Jeff saved him with a dry chuckle.

'Thought there was somethin' suspicious 'bout him just showin' up, but I'm glad he did. I ain't mad at you, Mark. You done me a favor, and I'm grateful,' Jeff said sincerely. 'Now, what 'bout somethin' to eat?'

'I could use a bite,' Mark admitted, and within a few minutes both men were digging into heaping plates of stew and pan bread, while they talked about old times as though they didn't have a care in the world.

★　　★　　★

Further out of town, Clint was tightening the cinch on the roan, and bidding the Claymores goodnight. His belly was full and he was feeling about as good as a man can who is living on borrowed time, and in a dangerous situation. He swung up into the saddle and glanced at Will and Shirley standing side by side on the wide veranda of the house. Will's hand rested protectively on Shirley's shoulder.

Clint lifted his hand and heard Shirley call, 'Be careful,' as he reined the roan away from the hitch rail.

'I will,' he answered. 'Thanks again for the hospitality.'

'Anytime, Clint,' Will replied.

Touching spurs to the roan, Clint put him into a canter and picked his way down the trail to the wagon road. The moon was just coming up, and the worn tracks of the path wound like a snake, showing slightly darker than the surrounding grass.

By the time he reached the gate and passed through, the moon was up and cast a clear, silvery light over the rocky roadway, making visibility extremely good. 'Too good,' Clint thought. From the ridges above, he knew that he stood out like a patch of black against a white background. It wasn't a comfortable feeling, but he felt certain that nobody knew where he was. He thought that he'd been extra careful about his backtrail, and although he rode cautiously, he was also confident that he was safe enough for the time being.

Glancing at the roan's ears, Clint almost missed their significance for several precious seconds. He had just rounded a slight curve in the road when Star's ears pointed directly toward a clump of boulders that were perched precariously on the slope of the hill.

Clint's sharp eyes caught the dark shadow moving between two of the large boulders. He was already beginning to roll from the saddle when a flash of fire erupted from a dark crack between the rocks. Something heavy smashed into his head and knocked his hat off, then he fell to the ground with a heavy thud and lay unmoving.

The roan stopped immediately, startled by the sudden way Clint had left the saddle and the rolling thunder of the rifle's sharp crack. Star turned back to the motionless rider lying on the road and smelled the blood dripping from the gash in Clint's head.

Fortunately, the roan placed himself in such a position that Bert Turner, who was rapidly reloading the single-shot Springfield rifle, couldn't fire again without hitting the horse, and if he did that, the horse would still fall in such a way as to block another shot at the downed rider.

Bert realized that he had scored a hit on Clint, and he instantly decided that the man was dead. The Springfield was a good rifle, sighted true and accurate, and Bert had centered directly on Clint's broad chest.

Suddenly filling with panic, Bert could think only of getting himself as far away from the scene as possible, and establishing himself some kind of an alibi. He knew that nothing so angered the western man as a back-shooter and dry-gulcher.

Hastily leaving his place of concealment, Bert clawed his way over the rocky side of the hill to where he had left his horse. Thrusting the rifle into the saddle scabbard, he mounted quickly and turned the horse toward Pine Creek. Nails had been avenged. 'It just goes to show,' Bert thought with satisfaction, 'no matter how fast a man is with a gun, there's always somebody capable of buying his meat.' He knew that Silk Barrister would pay a good penny for this news, and reward him well for getting rid of the troublemaker.

After arriving in town, Bert tied his horse to the string in back of Joe's, then shucked the saddle and hung it in the small shed in the rear. Entering the cafe-saloon, he had a drink as a toast to Nails. Then, after a second shot of whisky, he wiped his bearded mouth and headed for Barrister's store. But Silk wasn't there and the runt, McSweeny, wouldn't say where he was.

Bert bought himself a new bottle of whisky and returned to his dugout to drink himself into oblivion. He was unaware that at that moment Silk was meeting with his crew of ruffians to plan the morning attack on the Sweet Lady mine shack.

Barrister would have given a lot to have talked to Bert that night. Jackson's warning that morning had been clear, and Silk had no doubt that the gunman would fulfill his promise if he could. But Silk wasn't going to take any chances, and would always appear with his coat opened and no gun showing on him.

Even Clint Jackson would hesitate to shoot an unarmed man. But Silk wasn't unarmed. Strapped to his right forearm was a special spring-locked holster which held a deadly forty-one caliber single-shot derringer. A movement of the forearm muscles would release the holding catch, while another ingenious spring would catapult the gun downward into his waiting palm. Silk practiced, tensing the muscle in his arm tightly, and the small gun dropped like magic into his hand. To complete the movement, Silk thumbed the hammer back and took care not to touch the sensitive, unprotected trigger.

He lowered the hammer and slipped the gun under the sleeve of his jacket until the gun was locked into place. Silk knew he hadn't lost his touch, and smiled with satisfaction. If it came to a show-down between him and Jackson, he knew that Mr. Jackson just might have a surprise waiting for him; a very deadly surprise.

CHAPTER FOURTEEN

It was still dark when Jeff felt the heavy paw of Moses on his chest and felt the wolf's hot, panting breath on his face. Even in the extremely dim light from the coals of the fire, he could tell that Moses was tense and restless, the bristles on his back standing straight and stiff.

'Okay, boy,' Jeff said quietly to the wolf.

Jeff got up quickly. Without even taking the time to pull on his boots or slip up his suspenders, he moved quickly from rifle slot to rifle slot as he peered at the moonlit surroundings outside the cabin. Jeff could see nothing, but knew that Silk Barrister's men were out there in the darkness.

He woke Mark with a touch on his bony shoulder, and the old-timer came instantly awake. 'What is it, Jeff?' Mark asked alertly, and sat up on the side of the bunk bed.

'We got company, Mark. Those skunks are out there again. Best get dressed, 'less you want to go meet your Maker with your boots off,' Jeff sad quietly. He crossed to his own bed and sat down to pull on the high-topped boots that he favored.

Within minutes both men were peering out to the north and east, the most likely directions for an attack to come from. To the east was the timber pile, and the north was up-slope to higher ground, which is always favored by any attacking force.

It was still a while until dawn, so Jeff put on a pot of water to boil, even though he knew the extra smoke from the chimney would alert the men outside that they were up and probably ready for them. A man just isn't fit to face his Maker without a cup of hot coffee in his belly and a smoke to relax him. The two old men were too set in their ways to let an impending attack divert them from their simple pleasures.

'Mark, I think you ought to take the east slope, even though the sun'll be in your eyes, while I take the north slope with my Sharps,' Jeff said quietly as he sipped his coffee.

Then he told Mark of the defenses he and Clint had put out in case of an attack. 'As soon as the sun comes up, light this left-hand fuse. That'll give the polecats somethin' to think 'bout. It's only a dummy fuse, but they got no way of knowin' it. Meanwhile, I'll set off a charge of dynamite or two with my rifle on any skunk that tries to get close 'nuff to throw somethin' at us. Yep,' he said with a dry chuckle, 'I think those fellers are in for a rude awakenin'.'

'I sure hope so, Jeff,' Mark replied. 'Maybe if'n we make 'nuff noise Clint will hear it and come runnin'.'

'Maybe,' Jeff agreed, 'but let's don't count on it. No tellin' what the boy is a-doin'. 'Sides, we kin handle this little chore our own selves. Yep, a couple of salty old wolves like us can take care of this.'

The two men grinned at each other with good humor, then took up their respective stations while Moses paced the cabin, growling ominously.

★   ★   ★

Henry Barlow waited with a dozen men behind the pile of mining timbers. The men were making enough noise to wake up the dead with their scrambling over the rocks and gravel to get into position. Barlow had no hope that the man in the shack would be surprised, especially with the wolf in the shack with him. He didn't know that Mark Tollett was also in the cabin, but the knowledge would have made no difference in the plans. He knew that when the dynamite charges started exploding from the north slope, old Jeff was going to be too busy to notice the attack from the timber pile, especially since they would have the sun at their backs.

Barlow knew it was a good plan. All the men had to do was get up against the granite sides of the shack under the cover of the dynamite blasts, then fire inside ... if the place wasn't destroyed first. He figured that within an hour it would be all over one way or another.

He strained his eyes against the moonlit north slope and saw dark shapes of men moving from rock to rock, and from low spot to low spot as they edged closer to the mine shack. Barlow knew that all seven of the men on the north slope carried several charges of short-fused dynamite sticks. When the sun broke over the mountain, they had orders to light the fuses and toss the dynamite onto the roof of the shack.

Barlow knew that nothing in the world could withstand that kind of concussion, and he expected the shack to be flattened. Then there would be nothing left to do but clean up the mess. Still, it paid not to take any chances, and he was content to rely on Silk Barrister's specific orders about the attack.

He glanced at his watch and saw that it would be dawn in another fifteen minutes. It was very dark, but he knew that it was always darkest just before the dawn. Privately, he thought that that moment was the best time for the attack, but he wasn't running the show, only following orders.

Just as the minute hand on the watch

turned closer toward dawn, a loud, piercing scream broke the muffled silence of the night from the north slope. It was immediately followed by a second man screaming in great agony. Every man behind the timber pile instantly became alert and wondered what could have caused those men to cry out in such anguish and pain.

Since the element of surprise was lost, Barlow stood up and called in a loud voice: 'What's going on?'

One of the men on the north slope called back from the darkness: 'Ted Merk and Carl Rogers hurt themselves somehow.'

Sobbing cries came from above the shack, mixed with sounds of thrashing about on the gravel slope. Then another man yelled from the darkness: 'It's bear traps. I just found one set and waiting for me.'

'I'm getting the hell outta here,' yelled one of the men, instantly followed by another man yelling: 'Wait for me.'

Barlow called in a loud, gruff voice: 'Just hold on where you are. You're close enough to . . .'

The words were drowned out by the sharp crack of the Sharps rifle being fired from the shack. The shot was instantly followed by a powerful explosion when the heavy bullet slammed into a dynamite charge set in front of a marked boulder on the rocky north slope.

Rock, sand, rubble, and dust rained down on the men who were crouching on the north slope, lifting several of them in the air from the concussion of the blast. When the dust cleared, only five of the seven men staggered back up the slope. Two of those moved awkwardly in pain. One had the steel jaws of a bear trap clamped around one arm, and the other man was supported by a friend, since he had the steel jaws of a trap caught around his knee joint.

As the sun broke over the mountain, the men behind the timber pile could see a slightly blackened hole on the north slope. A small pile of loose rubble and one smoking boot were the only evidence of the two men who had been crouched behind the boulder only moments before.

As if that sight wasn't enough to take the heart out of the men, the next one put the twelve men behind the timber to flight. A steady stream of sparks and smoke wound its way toward the stack of timbers. The men instantly recognized it as a dynamite fuse that was burning rapidly and relentlessly toward their position.

Without hesitation, every man broke into a wild run back toward the Fancy Nance mine and the protection of the gully several dozen yards to the east. The sharp crack of the big Sharps rifle and the drowning roar of the double-barreled .12 gauge shotgun added wings to their booted feet.

One of the fleeing men stumbled and fell as a heavy lead ball from the Sharps rifle cut neatly through the fleshy cheeks of his buttocks. Barlow tried to stop their flight by grabbing one of the men. 'Shoot out the fuse!' Barlow yelled, but the only answer he received was a heavy blow on the mouth as the fear-crazed man fought his way clear of the timber pile.

Barlow picked himself up off the ground and glanced at the rapidly approaching smoke of the fuse, then left the pile himself. He knew there was no way that he could cut the fuse with a pistol or rifle shot. As he staggered away on heavy feet, a ball of lead from the Sharps rifle whistled past his ear like an angry hornet, and caused him to flinch and quicken his steps.

In the gully, Barlow lay with the other men waiting for the impending explosion, but it never came. After more than ten minutes, it dawned on the men that they had been horn-swaggled.

Barlow had been authorized by Barrister to offer more incentives if anything went wrong, so he raised his gruff voice for every man to hear.

'You let that old fool bluff you,' he cried loudly. 'The charge fizzled out. Mr. Barrister will pay an extra hundred for every man who will storm the shack and kill the old buzzard. Hell, he can't get all of us.'

The last statement wasn't exactly the kind of encouragement the men needed to hear, and there was some muttering among them.

'All right,' Barlow said, 'we can throw our own dynamite from the protection of the timber pile. It's only about sixty yards. Cameron, you got a good arm? How about you, Joe? Either one of you strong enough to throw a charge that far?'

The big ruffian, Joe Cooley, thought about it for a minute, then nodded. 'Yep, I might be able to do it. If not, then give me a cover of fire so I can get within thirty yards

247

of the shack.'

'Good!' Barlow replied with a false hardiness. 'Come on men, let's get back to the pile so Joe can try to throw a charge from there. If he can't, then we'll lay down a good cover of fire so he can get closer. Two hundred in gold for every man with guts.'

Then, to set an example, Barlow started out immediately, running in a low, criss-crossing crouch, and reached the safety of the timbers without a shot coming from the mine shack. Soon, another man followed him, then still more until there were eleven huddled in the safety of the heavy timbers. The only man who remained in the shallow gully was the one who had gotten shot in the buttocks.

The men knelt behind the pile and glanced through the cracks, only to see another fuse smoking and spewing sparks as it raced toward them. One man hollered in terror, then jumped up to run and was instantly knocked down by a heavy bullet from the shack. The man dropped as the bullet tore through his leg, and Barlow took advantage of the moment's confusion to shout.

'There ain't any dynamite. The old fool

is just trying to make us panic so he can get a clear shot.'

When the fuse sputtered out a few yards from the timber pile, the men drew a collective sigh of relief. Then, as Barlow was tying up a bundle of dynamite and sticking a short fuse in it, a third trail of smoke and sparks began its journey toward the pile of timbers.

Some of the men started firing into the cabin and a few shot at the fuse, but the shots only kicked up small mounds of dirt. It was evident that none of the men were gunslicks or marksmen.

The bullets glanced off the stone walls of the mine shack and ricocheted into the air with sharp, chilling sounds, yet no answering shots came from inside the shack. The fact emboldened several of the men, who began firing over the top of the timbers, setting up a rapid crescendo of shots at the rifle slots of the shack.

A pall of gunsmoke soon hung over the timber pile, and the stench of burnt gunpowder was heavy in the morning air. Still, the smoking fuse burned irrevocably closer with each passing second and a few of the men began to worry as it neared the timber pile.

One of the men, a little braver than the rest, jumped up on top of the pile and looked over to the other side. He saw for the first time the heap of newly dug rock and gravel at the bottom of the pile of heavy timbers.

Turning to the others, he shouted warningly: 'Run! There's a case of dynamite down there!' Jumping to the ground, the ruffian started a long-legged run toward the gully, and two other men tried to match strides with him. The three men had almost made it to the safety of the gully when the explosion came, and they were hurtled through the air like rag dolls from the force of the blast.

The earth seemed to tremble and quiver when the two cases of dynamite exploded. It shook the stone mining shack and was even felt deep inside the Fancy Nance and the other surrounding mines. The deafening sound rumbled down the valley and reverberated between the mountain peaks. For several minutes after the blast, the air appeared full of flying debris: timbers, rocks, gravel, and dirt.

When the pall of dust finally cleared away, all that remained were a few articles of clothes which were smoking and burned, a few boots, some of which still contained the ghastly remains of the men who had worn them, and some twisted pieces of steel and splintered wood that had been weapons only a short time before. Four bodies were later recovered and buried on boot hill in unmarked graves.

In the cabin below, Jeff couldn't restrain a wild Texas 'yippie' when he saw the destruction that had been vented on his enemies. Jeff and Mark danced around inside the shack holding onto each other's shoulders and laughed until they were weak. But after a few minutes, both men got quiet and felt a little ashamed at having such joyous feelings from the death of so many men.

Mark summed up the feelings of both of them when he said soberly: 'Old Jeff, I think Silk Barrister is goin' to have a bit of trouble findin' men to do his dirty chores from now on.'

Jeff nodded his head in agreement, and said quietly: 'Yep, I bet he sure will.'

★   ★   ★

Dozens of men poured out of the Fancy Nance and other mines along the rocky slope, looking with wonder at the scene of death and destruction. A few took off their hats in silent homage to the dead, but most of the men felt a surge of gratitude that the scum had finally gotten their just desserts.

The night crews had felt the power of the blast in the underground tunnels and had climbed to the surface to see what had caused it. Later, when the day shift arrived at the mines, they too could only stare in awe and listen to the stories from the few who had seen the whole fight.

Still, no one tried to approach the Sweet Lady mine shack. They were not only ashamed that they had stood aside while an old man fought the battle alone, but also were unsure as to what kind of a reception they would meet. The men stood around talking in awe and wonder about old Jeff, and a holiday was called by the foremen of the mines without even consulting the owners.

CHAPTER FIFTEEN

Clint lay unmoving on the roadbed for hours, the roan standing a lonely vigil. Star knew that Clint was alive, even though he had the frightening odor of blood on him. After a long time, Clint stirred slightly and Star stooped over and breathed heavily on him.

The action caused Clint's eyes to flutter open as he fought his way into consciousness. Waves of pain turned into red sheets as flashing comets appeared before his eyes. A sharp, throbbing pain assaulted his head. He felt himself becoming physically sick and turned his head to empty his fluttering stomach of its contents.

Clint knew that he was hurt badly. Each time he opened his eyes, he saw the big roan and the surrounding hills and trees. Everything was spinning as though he were on a rope-swing like he'd done as a boy.

Clint had to use the stirrup of the saddle to pull himself to his feet. He found that he didn't have the strength to mount the saddle, and could only cling weakly to the iron saddle horn. He wrapped his elbow joint around the saddle horn and leaned against the roan as he tried to stop his head from spinning with such sickening speed.

With the aid of Star, he started shakily down the trail. His vision was blurred and unfocused, and Clint prayed that the impairment of his sight wasn't permanent. If it was, he knew that he would rather have been killed back on the road. Finally the ground and his surroundings quit spinning long enough for him to recognize a small animal path leading up the mountainside. He turned the roan onto it and almost lost his hold on the saddle as the roan climbed in irregular spurts, half dragging Clint up the rocky trail.

Getting off the trail, he stopped the roan in a clump of brush and sluggishly untied the saddle-bags. Then he sank down wearily against a large boulder, fighting the waves of nausea and dizziness that threatened to engulf him. Clint slept fitfully throughout the night, slipping into unconsciousness shortly before sunrise.

While Clint fought his battle for life on the ledge overlooking the wagon road, Cole Neyland was already up and watching the activity at the Claymore ranch. The hands had risen before daylight and staggered sleepily to the cook-shack for breakfast. After getting orders from the foreman, they rode out of the yard to do the day's work at the ranch.

Cole could see the lights come on in the

big house. Right after dawn, Will Claymore saddled his horse and left to take care of ranch business before heading into town to supervise the mining operations.

As far as Cole could tell, there was nobody at the ranch except the two cooks and Shirley Claymore. He knew there would never be a better time than now if he moved quickly. He figured that he could be in the house and have her out before anyone knew about it.

Quickly throwing the saddle on his horse, Cole broke camp and mounted up. Then he headed down the hillside and into the meadow behind the corrals. He approached unseen and unheard over the thick grass, and, within minutes, he was mounting the stairs to the second floor of the house.

Cole paused outside what he believed to be Shirley's bedroom. As he glanced through the window, he couldn't see anything in the darkened room. Silently, he tried the handle of the door, and, as expected, it opened. Entering, he paused to let his eyes adjust to the darkness.

He saw a canopied bed covered with light muslin curtains. Cole approached it cautiously, but some sixth sense seemed to alert the bed's occupant. A soft sleepy voice said: 'Is that you, Will dear?'

Cole didn't dare reply, so he quickened his steps across the room and reached the bed just as Shirley rose up in faint alarm. He saw that she was dressed in a flimsy nightgown and that her long blonde hair flowed freely about her shoulders.

'Will, say something!' Shirley said, fully awake. Then she gasped as the curtains parted violently and a gloved hand grabbed her in an iron grip, choking off the scream in her throat before it could carry.

The fingers of steel tightened their hold on her throat. Although she fought with all her strength, she couldn't breathe and the fingers were cutting off the flow of blood to her brain. Slowly the struggle became weaker, then quit altogether as she passed into unconsciousness.

When she went limp in his hands, Cole loosened the tight grip and felt Shirley take a ragged, gasping breath. After he was sure that she was unconscious and still alive, he tore the muslin curtains down and ripped them into strips.

Working quickly, Cole tied her hands behind her back, then tied her ankles together, and put a thick gag in her mouth.

256

After checking that she was well bound, he lifted her across his shoulders and left the room quickly and quietly.

Back in the meadow, he lifted her onto the bow of the saddle, then swung himself onto the seat. Cole pulled Shirley across his thighs and lap, then headed the horse into the tree line of the surrounding hills just as dawn broke. The dense foliage shielded them from the cook who had just entered the yard to fetch a bucket of water from the well near the stables.

Cole guided the horse around the trail leading from the ranch to the wagon road, and came out on the roadway a half mile from the turn off. He hoped that he wouldn't meet anybody on the road. If he did, he would have to kill them to keep his identity a secret.

Putting the horse into a fast canter, he headed down the wagon road toward the cabin where he intended to keep Shirley for a while. It was now full light and Shirley stirred, then began to struggle. Cole was forced to use one hand to keep her from wiggling off the saddle.

'Bitch, keep it up and I'll knock you out again,' he warned, giving her a hard slap across her shapely buttocks, which brought a muffled protest from her. Then she lay still, knowing that there was little hope of fighting from the position that she was in.

Fortunately, the struggle occurred at the exact spot where Clint had lain bleeding during the night. Cole didn't see the bloody disheveled figure on a rocky ledge several hundred feet above the trail.

But Clint spotted Cole Neyland pass by carrying a white burden across the saddle bow. The scene appeared unreal to Clint, and blurred, but by closing one eye, he was finally able to recognize the horse, rider and the figure across the saddle. He realized that Cole Neyland was kidnapping Shirley, and that she was practically naked in a flimsy white nightgown. He assumed that she had been snatched from her bed.

A wave of sickness prevented him from firing a shot at Cole, and before he recovered, the tall, dark gunman had disappeared from sight.

Working with shaking hands, Clint opened the saddle bag and pulled out a bandana, then tied it tightly around his head and shoved his battered hat into the bag. With slow movements, he struggled to his feet, staggered to the roan and pulled himself heavily onto the saddle. Then, using both hands to hang onto the saddle horn, he used his body weight and the stirrups to guide the roan down the trail to the road. Anything above a walk jarred him so much that he came close to passing out from the pain, so he had to content himself with the slower pace as he hung onto the saddle horn to keep his seat.

By keeping one eye closed, Clint managed to follow the deep tracks of the double-mounted horse. His muddled mind could picture the small cabin in the narrow valley that he had passed the day before and it suddenly dawned on him why two of Barrister's men were in possession of the place.

Minutes later, Clint came to the almost invisible trail that led to the cabin and he saw that Cole had turned off onto it.

Clint followed the tracks and went the same way as he had gone the day before. He circled the cabin and came in at the small stream. He dismounted and ducked his throbbing head under the surface of the water, feeling the cold iciness of it clear his head. After drinking deeply to quench his thirst and relieve his parched throat, he ducked his head once again in the water and let the numbing coldness wash away some of the pain.

Rising from the stream, Clint almost felt like his old self once again, and his vision was vastly improved. He stood without swaying and pulled the new Marlin forty-four caliber rifle from the scabbard that was tied under the saddle skirt, and jacked a shell in the chamber. Clint left the roan standing in the stream and went up the stream bank until he sighted the cabin.

Clint saw the two men who had been there the day before. They were standing outside the cabin, and were having words with Cole Neyland, who was holding Shirley by her upper arm. He noticed that her feet had been untied, and the gown she wore did nothing to cover her lovely body from the men's eyes. The bearded man was having hot words with Cole, but the other one was standing off to the side and was looking at Shirley with lust-filled eyes.

After a moment, the bearded man began to stomp away toward the corral, but was brought up short by Cole's hard voice. Then Neyland calmly pulled one of his six-guns and held it pointed at the man's back.

The bearded man turned and looked at Cole for a long minute, then turned his back and started walking away. Cole thumbed the six-gun and Clint saw the flame spout from the barrel. When the heavy slug slammed into the man's back, he flung out his arms and crumpled to the ground where he lay unmoving in the grass.

Clint dropped to the ground behind a small clump of weeds and brought the rifle sight into line. Clint knew what Cole and the other man intended to do with Shirley, besides hold her for some kind of ransom. Apparently the other man had rebelled against the plan and tried to leave, but Cole had ruthlessly gunned him down.

Once they got Shirley into the cabin, Clint knew that he wouldn't be able to get them out without some help. Knowing that he had little choice in the matter, Clint sighted in on Cole Neyland's left shoulder. Then, just as his finger tightened on the trigger, Shirley jerked away, almost getting free, and Cole moved slightly. He stiffened as the heavy forty-four slug caught him in the center of the back and dropped him to the ground as though he'd been pole-axed. Cole lay unmoving on the ground; the bullet had sliced through his spine, yet had missed all his vital organs.

Shirley used the moment's confusion to turn and run as the crack of the rifle shot reverberated in the still air. The other man made a wild lunge for her while at the same time he drew his pistol and fired a quick shot in Clint's direction.

Quickly jacking another shell in the rifle, Clint compensated for the bullet's drop on the unsighted rifle and squeezed the trigger again. The bullet caught the man high in the right shoulder and caused the gun to fall from his numb fingers. He stopped and looked around wildly as he held the shattered shoulder. All thought of Shirley was forgotten as searing pain coursed through him.

Then he turned and ran toward the cabin door and Clint fired again, hitting him in the leg and dropping him heavily to the ground on the bullet-torn shoulder. The man lay still, afraid to move in fear that it might bring another bullet.

'Don't shoot! Don't shoot! I'm hurt!' he called loudly.

Cole Neyland was lying motionless, yet was conscious of what was happening around him. He couldn't move his body because he was paralyzed from the waist down and too stunned to reach for his gun. Surprisingly, there was little pain, just a kind of numbness. Unable to move, Cole could only lay and wait to see who had fired the deadly shot.

Shirley saw Clint rise and she hurried toward him, unaware of the mouth-watering sight she was even for a man in his condition. Her unbound breasts jiggled tantalizingly under the thin fabric of her nightgown. Within a minute she was in his arms, sobbing and shaking hysterically.

Taking the Spanish knife from a hip scabbard, he cut the bonds on her wrists and held her reassuringly in his arms. A sharp whistle brought Star from the stream and he slipped the blanket roll from behind the saddle and wrapped her within its folds.

After putting the rifle back in the saddle scabbard, he asked quietly, 'Did he hurt you?'

'He ... he choked me ... and ... and hit me,' she sobbed. 'That other man ... they were going to ... oh, it's so horrible,' she said, crying against his shoulder.

'Stay here a minute,' Clint said gently. 'I'll be right back.'

Drawing the pistol, Clint approached the two downed men cautiously. The one who had tried to shoot him was moaning openly from the pain of his wounds and looking fearfully at the sight of the big pistol in

Clint's hand.

'Please, mister,' he whined.

'Shut up,' Clint snapped with controlled anger as he turned to Cole Neyland and removed the left-hand gun from its holster. He saw that it was a Colt peacemaker, forty-five caliber, perfectly balanced with a five-inch barrel.

With his face bathed in sweat, Cole looked up at Clint and said with a sneer: 'You've crippled me, Jackson. Put another bullet in me and end it.'

'Not me, Cole,' he replied. 'It seems like kind'a poetic justice to leave you just like you are.'

'Damn you, Jackson,' he hissed, 'you did it to me, so at least have the decency to finish the job.'

'Cole, I only meant to put a bullet in your shoulder. I wasn't tryin' to kill you. You're goin' to have to make up your own mind 'bout your life. The best I can do, Cole, is leave the decision up to you.'

Clint shucked out four loads of Cole's pistol and left only one in the cylinder, then tossed the gun close to him so he could reach it. Looking down at the gunfighter, he said quietly: 'Cole, the choice is yours. I'll send a doctor back if you change your mind. Then you can hang for this.'

'What about me?' the other man asked as he stared at Clint.

'Be here when the posse comes and you'll swin' from a tree. If'n I was you, I'd find a way to fork a horse and wouldn't stop 'til I was across the Rio Grande,' Clint said coldly.

Turning on his heel, Clint walked back to the roan and mounted, then helped Shirley get up behind him on the saddle. She tightened the blanket around her and clung to his belt as he turned the roan back to the trail leading to the wagon road.

Idly, Clint speculated on what Cole Neyland's decision would be. There was no doubt in his own mind as to what he would have done in Cole's place. He found himself listening for the sound of the gunshot, which finally came just as he topped the ridge leading out of the valley.

Within minutes, Clint turned the roan back up the road to the Five-star ranch to return Shirley to the man she loved. There was no one around the house when they rode into the yard, so Clint dismounted and helped her down from the back of the horse.

'Shirley, you can tell your husband 'bout

this if'n you've a mind to,' Clint said quietly. 'But no matter what you decide to do, not a word of what happened will ever pass my lips.'

'Thank you, Clint,' she replied softly. 'You have become more than a friend and I will always be in your debt.'

'No, there's no debt in this matter. You and Will don't owe me a thin'.' Then he added, 'Right now I've got some unfinished business with Silk Barrister. He put Cole Neyland up to that.'

'But, your head ... you're hurt!'

'I'm all right now.'

'Then be careful, Clint, he's a dangerous man,' she cautioned.

'If'n he won't draw, then I'll just have to use my fists on him and run him outta Pine Creek once and for all,' Clint vowed. 'Now you get in the house a'fore somebody sees you and spreads the word.'

'I will, and thank you, Clint,' she said, and quickly walked up the steps and into the house.

Clint mounted and turned the roan as he started once more for town. There was a grim resolve in his gray eyes, and his lips were hard and unsmiling. He knew that it was time to take care of Silk Barrister once and for all.

CHAPTER SIXTEEN

Back in Pine Creek, Silk Barrister heard the explosions of dynamite reverberating from the mountainsides and felt a deep satisfaction, but his joy only lasted until the first stragglers came into town. It was the two who had been badly injured by bear traps.

The satisfaction turned into bile as Silk listened to the results of the fiasco at the Sweet Lady mine. A grim foreboding came over him as he thought of what would happen when Clint Jackson found out about the latest thrust at the mine.

Silk quickly went to his office and started stuffing his papers and cash into a canvas valise, preparing to leave town until the heat died down. McSweeny stuck his head in the door and said that Bert Turner wanted to talk to him.

With an impatient gesture, he told McSweeny to let Turner in as he stuck the bag under the desk and closed the iron safe. It wouldn't do for Turner to know that he was fixing to pull up stakes. He would tell only McSweeny, who would carry on in his absence.

Bert appeared in the doorway looking disheveled and dirty, the once-white bandage covering his mutilated ear. He looked both sullen and triumphant, and almost gloated when he thought about the wonderful news that he had for the boss.

'Well, what is it, Bert?' Silk demanded impatiently. 'I'm pretty busy right now, so make it quick.'

'Boss, you know that troublemaker, Clint Jackson?' Bert asked.

'Of course I know him. What about him?' Silk asked quietly as he fought to hold down his anger.

'Well, boss, I took care of him last night,' Bert said, grinning, his eyes gleaming.

'Took care of him? How? Bert, tell me what you are talking about and quit beating around the bush,' Silk said as he leaned half way out of his chair.

'I shot him, boss, and left him for dead on the wagon road by the Claymore ranch.'

'Are you sure?' Silk asked, not believing the news. 'Did you put a bullet in his head?'

Bert shifted uncomfortably, then said: 'Well, boss, I saw him hit and I watched him fall. He didn't move, so he's dead all right. I couldn't get a second shot at him because his horse got in my way, so I came on back to town.'

'Go back,' Silk hissed angrily. 'Bring me his gun. Bring me that big cannon he carries so I will know you got him and I'll give you a thousand dollars. And Bert, if you didn't kill him, just keep on riding, or I'll kill you with my bare hands.'

'Sure boss, sure. The gun . . . I'll get it,' he said hastily. Then, feeling confident that Jackson was dead, he said in an arrogant voice: 'You just have that money ready when I get back.'

Bert strode clumsily to the door and pulled it shut behind him. Silk sat back with relief. If only it was true, then he wouldn't have to flee as he had done so many times in the past. Even if Jackson wasn't dead, he was shot, making him easy pickings for Cole Neyland.

Silk knew that he needed to get Cole back into town in case Jackson did show up. But Cole would probably still be at the Claymore ranch waiting for a chance to snatch Shirley, unless he had already done it. If that was the case, then he would be at the cabin, or maybe already back in town.

With all those thoughts running through his mind, Silk sat back in the chair and relaxed. Then he told McSweeny to send a man to find Cole and tell him to get back to town. After McSweeny scurried out, Silk poured himself a stiff shot of whisky and thought that just maybe things would work themselves out yet.

When the early morning explosions reverberated through the valley, Mary and Kevin looked at each other in fearful alarm. They knew that usually the dynamite blasts weren't heard so far from the mines, and apprehension clutched them both at the same time.

'The Sweet Lady!' Mary whispered, but Kevin could not answer because his throat was so tight.

'Kevin, saddle me a horse,' she ordered firmly. 'I have to go find out what happened.'

'I'll go, sis,' he replied at last. 'You know that you can't ride a horse in a dress.'

'Hurry then,' she urged. 'Saints preserve us, I hope it's nothing.'

Kevin worked quickly saddling the horse, and within a few minutes he was driving spurless heels into the fat flanks of the stable mare.

When he arrived at the Sweet Lady a short time later, Kevin took in the scene of total destruction, but his young mind couldn't fit pictures of what he saw to the actual happenings. It was with a sigh of relief that he saw the mine shack was still standing, and he reined the mare up the steep slope. Kevin dismounted just as Jeff opened the door. He looked from the old man to Mark and saw the grins on their wrinkled faces.

'What's your hurry, youngster?' Mark asked in good humor.

'Me and Mary was worried about you, Mr. Tollett,' he replied, then added, 'You too, Uncle Jeff.'

'Boy, who you unclin' 'round here?' Jeff asked with mock fierceness. 'I ain't your uncle.'

Kevin looked abashed for a moment, and said: 'Well, you're Clint's uncle, and I wasn't thinking, I guess.'

'That's okay, boy, you can call me Uncle Jeff if'n you've a mind to,' he said with a chuckle.

'Come on in,' Mark invited and stood aside.

Kevin entered the cabin and pulled up short at the sight of the fray-coated bundle of fierceness who was called Moses. Kevin's eyes lit up at seeing the doglike creature at close range. Without fear or hesitation, he walked over to Moses and, with a casual gesture, he rested his hand on the broad back of the wolf.

Neither of the men had been paying any attention, and when Mark turned around and saw Kevin, his blood turned to ice water. He watched with wonder while the wolf demurely submitted to the ear scratching.

'Well, I'll be a monkey's uncle,' Mark said softly.

Jeff finished barring the door, then turned and saw what was happening. The boy was the first person that Moses had ever allowed to touch him besides himself. He felt a pang of jealousy surge through him, but managed to keep from showing it so as not to upset the wolf.

'You fixin' to spoil my dog, boy?' Jeff asked gruffly. 'That's a man-eatin' wolf there, least he was 'til he met up with a fool boy that don't have 'nuff sense to be scared of him.'

'I'm sorry, Uncle Jeff,' Kevin said

hastily. 'I wasn't trying to spoil him for you, honest.' Yet his fingers kept working their magic on the wolf's ears.

'Well, see that you don't.' Jeff replied with a snort.

'Mr. Tollett, what happened here?' Kevin asked. 'I've got to get back. Mary's worried sick about you and Clint hasn't come back either.'

Jeff slapped his hands together and picked up his Sharps rifle, and said: 'Mark, you tell him. I'm goin' to borrow your horse and get into town. That is, if'n you'll keep an eye on things for a while.'

'You think you ought to, Jeff?' Mark asked.

'Yep, it's the last thin' in the world they'll be expectin' me to do. 'Sides, with you here, they won't be able to get close to the mine. That is, if'n they've still got the heart for it,' Jeff said with a devilish grin.

'Well, go ahead then, you old fool,' Mark said with a snort. 'Don't worry 'bout the Lady. I'll guard her like she's my own.'

Jeff put some long brass cartridges into his pocket while Mark unbarred the door. Then, with a touch on his friend's shoulder, Jeff let himself and Moses out of the shack. He mounted the mare, reined it

273

around, and went down the side of the slope toward town with the gray wolf loping alongside.

Stopping at the livery stable, he saw Mary, and after he dismounted, Jeff assured her that everything was all right at the mine.

'Uncle Jeff, what about Clint?' Mary asked worriedly. 'He has been gone all night and there hasn't been a word about him since he left to visit the Claymore ranch early yesterday afternoon.'

'Girl, I ain't seen hide nor hair of him,' Jeff admitted quietly. 'Right now, I've got some pressin' business with Silk Barrister, but I got to admit that I'm more inclined to look into what's happened to that youngster. If'n anythin' has happened to my nephew, Silk Barrister won't live to see another sunrise on this green earth,' he vowed soberly.

Mary suddenly turned pale white at those words, and Jeff immediately regretted causing her more worry. He patted her on the arm in an awkward gesture.

'Don't you worry none, girl. That youngster can take care of himself pretty good. It ain't likely that any skunk can get the best of him, no matter what,' Jeff said with more assurance in his voice than he felt. He knew that any man could be dry-gulched.

'Oh! Uncle Jeff, he's only a man,' she replied quietly. 'I'm so worried that I just can't seem to think straight. Please go find him for me,' she pleaded softly.

'Girl, I got the feelin' that you're kind'a stuck on the boy,' Jeff said gently.

'Yes Uncle Jeff,' she said pridefully, lifting her small chin. 'I love him. Will you please find him for me and make sure that he is all right?'

Jeff studied her young, pretty face for a moment, and liked her Irish pride and beauty. He said quietly: 'Sure will, girl.' Then, to take her mind off of Clint, he asked her unnecessarily for the directions to the Claymore ranch. After he made her repeat them twice, he mounted up and left by the back door of the barn.

★　　　★　　　★

After leaving Shirley at the ranch, Clint returned to the spot where he'd been ambushed and took a long look around the rocks that had concealed the bushwhacker.

275

Recovered from the head wound, he dismounted and climbed the hillside, searching for signs of the culprit.

Clint saw some boot tracks in the dirt behind the boulders, then he found a couple of cigarette stubs, an empty whisky bottle, and a brass cartridge casing. He picked up the casing and saw that it was a .44–.70, which was a common enough shell for a single shot Army carbine or a Springfield rifle. He slipped it into his shirt pocket and eased back down the hill.

He had just mounted the roan when Bert Turner came around the bend in the road and abruptly pulled his horse to a halt. Clint eyed the bearded man with weary suspicion, and saw the surprise and confusion on Bert's face when their eyes met. The dark scowling eyes looked nervously toward the ambush site. Clint instantly knew that Bert was the one who had bushwhacked him. He sensed that Bert knew he'd guessed the play.

Tensing with fear, Bert held the reins of the horse directly at his waist where the butt of the forty-one caliber revolver brushed against his hand. The heavy coat he wore and the horse's head concealed the gun from Clint's view and Bert knew that he had the element of surprise on his side if only he could pull the gun. Silk Barrister would pay him a thousand dollars for Jackson's hide, and he had no intention of passing up money like that, not after muffing the job the night before. He saw that Jackson's eyes were riveted on the rifle resting in the saddle scabbard.

Bert knew that turning and making a run for it would be a dead give-away of his guilt, and since he wasn't a good shot with a pistol, he decided to bluff his way out of the situation.

Nudging the horse forward, he said gruffly: 'You fixin' to hog the whole road, Jackson?'

'Turner,' Clint said evenly in his low, cold voice. 'I don't know what you're doin' out this way, but I got a pretty good idea. If'n you want some good advice, I'd say to just keep right on ridin'. There ain't nothin' for you in Pine Creek except a ration of hot lead.'

'I don't take advice from you, Jackson,' he replied, stopping his horse a dozen yards from where Clint sat on the roan.

'Well Turner, be that as it may,' Clint said coldly. 'I'm on my way into town to take care of your boss, Silk Barrister, and when I get through with him, I'm goin' to start buryin' scum like you. I got a hunch it was you who ambushed me last night, but I'm not in the mood right now to take care of you. If'n you keep on ridin' out of the country, I might just forget it. If'n you don't, Turner, the next time I see you, I'll kill you or else shoot you up so bad that you'll wish you were dead.'

Bert flushed with anger. His fingers closed around the butt of the revolver and he got a good grip on it as he glared hotly at Clint.

'Turner, Cole Neyland cashed in his chips a while ago. If'n you pull that iron, you'll die right here, then lay on this road 'til you rot,' Clint said dispassionately. 'My advice is to pull it out left-handed and drop it on the road along with that rifle, then ride while you still have breath left in your body.'

Bert's confidence suddenly crumpled and a hand of fear clutched his heart. If Cole Neyland didn't stand a chance, then he surely didn't. Here he was with his hand already on his gun and Jackson sat with his hand on his saddle, yet he was completely assured and unafraid. Clint's cold gray eyes remained unwavering and his face was set in hard lines.

Suddenly, Bert knew that if he tried to pull his gun on Clint, he would be a dead man. Life suddenly seemed more precious to him than it had ever been. His shoulders slumped and he expelled a long breath of air like a shudder. Then he said quietly: 'Okay Jackson, you win.'

Spreading his fingers wide to show that they were empty, he reached across and pulled the pistol with his left hand and dropped it on the ground. Then, reaching forward, he slipped the rifle out of the scabbard and let it fall to the dirt.

'Turner, ride on,' Clint said evenly. 'Don't stop 'til you're outta this country, and don't ever cross my trail again.'

Bert dug his spurs into the horse and passed Clint without a glance. When he rounded the next curve, he whipped the horse viciously with the reins and spurs as he took his frustration and anger out on the dumb beast.

Clint waited until Bert was out of sight, then he swung down from the saddle and scooped up the rifle and pistol. He stuck the pistol in the waistband of his pants, remounted the roan and held the rifle across his knees. Touching spurs to the roan, Clint started on for town for his showdown with Silk Barrister. It was long past time to take care of the snake, Clint thought grimly.

CHAPTER SEVENTEEN

A short distance from town, Clint pulled the roan to a stop and was surprised to see his uncle riding toward him with Moses loping easily alongside. He waited for the old man to pull up and took note of the big Sharps lying across the saddle bow.

'Uncle Jeff, what're you doin' out here?' Clint asked curiously. 'I thought you were goin' to stay holed up in the mine?'

'Was,' he replied gruffly, 'but I got to worryin' 'bout you, boy. Me and that redheaded gal of yours.'

'Mary?'

'Humph,' he snorted. 'How many redheaded gals you got, boy?'

'Actually Uncle Jeff, I ain't got any.'

'Yep, well don't be too sure 'bout that. That little Irisher figures a mite different 'bout it. Right cute she is, too,' Jeff said with a chuckle.

Clint shrugged impatiently, not liking the direction of the conversation. Then he asked: 'What 'bout the mine? Did you leave Mark there by himself?'

'Yep, him and Kevin. But he can handle it after the whuppin' we gave the polecats,' he said, chuckling. Then he gave Clint a full account of the fight at the mine that morning.

'Boy, what have you been doin', 'sides gettin' yourself shot,' Jeff said. 'Better not say you've been makin' cow-eyes at the Claymore woman,' he warned, and added with humor, 'if'n you have, that redhead might get a mite mad.'

'Nope, although that's a lot of woman to make eyes at, Uncle Jeff,' Clint replied with a smile. Then he filled Jeff in on all that had happened since their last meeting, ending the tale with his letting Bert Turner ride away.

'That was a damn fool thin' to do, boy. You should have killed the slimy snake,' Jeff said positively. 'How's your head now?'

'It seems to be all right, Uncle Jeff. Had me worried for a spell, but I'm fine now.'

'Well, boy, what're you plannin' to do?' he asked, and watched Clint with sharp eyes.

'I'm goin' to finish my talk with Barrister,' he replied. 'I gave him warnin' and he didn't take it, so now he's goin' to pay the piper.'

'Yep, thought you'd say that,' Jeff said gruffly. 'But I don't think he'll ever pull on you, boy.'

'Then I'll just have to give him the beatin' of his life and run him outta town,' Clint said evenly. 'A good stompin' and he'll be ready to pull up stakes.'

'Maybe,' Jeff said noncommitally, and they turned the horses toward town. 'What 'bout afterwards? You made any plans yet?'

'No, Uncle Jeff. Guess I'll be riding on. I don't think minin' is for me after all,' Clint said as he watched the wolf lope alongside the horses.

'Ridin' on!' Jeff said with scorn. 'Dan' fool, you wantin' to cut out on me just when I'll be needin' you the worst. Leavin' that little gal all in tears too. If'n that ain't gratitude for you,' Jeff snapped gruffly.

'What're you talkin' 'bout, Uncle Jeff?' Clint asked as he looked at the old man. 'Once Silk Barrister is out of the way, then there ain't nothin' holdin' me here. 'Sides, I ain't known that girl but three days,' he added.

'Humph, you got a lot to learn 'bout women, boy,' Jeff said with a snort. 'Who's gonna run the Sweet Lady? Who's gonna ramrod my minin' outfit while I'm away in Europe? Here I let you muscle in on my fun and when the fun's over you're gonna pull out and leave me with all the work?' Jeff said, sounding aggrieved.

'What're you talkin' 'bout, Uncle Jeff?' Clint asked, while he eyed the old man sharply. 'That's your mine and your gold. It ain't none of mine.'

'Boy, that's where you're wrong,' he replied. 'You're my partner. You're kin, and all the kin-folks are gonna get a share of the mine. I got you down for ten percent 'cause you're gonna run the thin' for me and handle all the troublesome details. Nope, you can't run out on me, boy,' he said firmly.

Clint was speechless for several minutes. Never had he ever heard of such a generous offer. That mine was worth maybe a million dollars and here his uncle was offering him ten percent for doing something that he could hire a man to do for sixty a month. It took some deep thought and a bit of getting used to.

'I don't know, Uncle Jeff,' Clint replied finally.

'Boy, just don't say "no" right off the bat. Think on it a spell,' Jeff said shrewdly. 'Of course, I got one condition, though.'

'Yep,' Clint said with a grin. 'I thought so. What is it?'

'Just this. You call your first boy Jefferson after me, and don't give him no middle name to use instead. You sure 'nuff disappointed me when you used Clinton instead of Jefferson.'

'I didn't do it with that in mind, Uncle Jeff. It seems like one Jeff in the family at a time is 'nuff,' he said.

'Well, I ain't gonna be 'round forever, boy, and I sort of like to think of my name stayin' 'round after I'm gone.'

'If'n I accept the deal, all right, and if'n I don't and ever have a son, I'll still call him Jeff after you.'

'Fair 'nuff,' Jeff agreed quickly with a smile, then added, 'Well, there it is, Barrister's tradin' post. Looks kind'a deserted, don't it?'

'Yep, but I doubt if it is, unless he got smart and headed outta the country.'

'Don't worry 'bout nothin', boy. I'm backin' your play with this big cannon here,' Jeff said and chuckled.

'All right, Uncle Jeff, but let me take care of Silk.'

'He's your meat, boy. Bury him deep.'

At the hitching rail beside the store they dismounted and Clint took up a position directly in front of the porch facing the doorway. Jeff stood a few paces away and off to one side. He held the Sharps rifle in the crook of his arm, cocked and with his finger on the trigger as his eyes swept all the doorways on the street.

'Barrister! Silk Barrister!' Clint called loudly for the whole town to hear. 'Get out here, we got an argument that ain't finished yet!'

Suddenly, the fronts of tents were crowded with miners who had been let off of work for the day. It seemed that the whole town spilled out into the street to see what was happening at the trading post.

Inside the store, McSweeny looked nervously out the front window, then hurried back to the office and burst inside without knocking.

Silk was just putting on his hat; the canvas valise was on the desk. He was debating the chances of getting out of town through the back door, but knew he had

285

waited too long. Too many men had failed him. Now he knew that he stood alone.

'He's outside again, Mr. Barrister,' McSweeny said, standing in the doorway rubbing his hands together nervously.

'Yes, I heard him, McSweeny,' Silk said kindly as he pulled on his hat. As an afterthought, he said to McSweeny: 'If this don't come out right, then all this is yours.'

Without waiting for a reply, Silk went through the door and into the front part of the store. As he reached the front door, he unbuttoned his coat and stepped out on the porch. After pulling the door shut, he turned to face Clint and spread his coat wide to show that he carried no gun.

'Jackson, I'm not armed. Shoot me and you're a murderer,' Silk said in a loud voice so everyone could hear.

'Silk Barrister, you're through in Pine Creek,' Clint said coldly as his eyes glittered with anger. 'There's more'n one way to skin a skunk. Since you don't have the nerve to pull on me, then I'm goin' to see if'n I can beat you to death with my fists. You're finished, Barrister.'

'I've killed men with my bare hands, Jackson,' he replied in a low voice.

'Maybe,' Clint agreed, 'but it must have

been a long time ago. You ain't never goin'
to sic Cole Neyland on nobody again. Also,
the other two who were with him, and
Turner, ain't comin' back either.'

Silk's face turned chalky white at the
words. No matter what happened now, he
knew that he was finished in Pine Creek for
good. If Jackson didn't kill him, then the
miners and ranchers would; especially Will
Claymore. They would hang him from the
nearest tree.

His dark eyes turned cold as he glared
malevolently at Clint, who he blamed for
his downfall. Silk burned with a hatred that
knew no bounds. If nothing else, he was
determined to kill Clint with his own hands
before he cashed in his chips.

Clint reached down and untied the thong
on the holster on his right leg as his left
hand reached for the belt buckle. For a
second he took his eyes off of Silk, and that
second cost him.

Taking advantage of the split second,
Silk flexed his arm and the Derringer
dropped into his waiting palm. In one
quick motion the small gun was cocked just
as Jeff yelled a warning.

'Look out, Clint! He's packin'!'

The shout came a second too late as fire

287

and smoke belched from the barrel of the Derringer in Silk's hand. Clint, caught off guard, felt a heavy blow strike him in the midsection. It felt like a mule kick and he went down, stunned and with the wind knocked out of him, as a sharp burning sensation raced along his ribs.

At the same instant, the muzzle of the big Sharps lined up on Silk's chest and Jeff's finger tightened on the trigger. Silk dropped the Derringer and screamed at Jeff: 'I'm not armed!'

'You said that a'fore you slimy snake,' Jeff said, and felt the heavy rifle buck like a mule in his hands.

The bullet caught Silk under the chin, moving upward, and blew out the back of his head along with his hat. The heavy slug lifted him violently into the air and hurled him backward where he crashed into the store. Silk was dead before the roar of the shot had died away.

Dropping the rifle in the street, Jeff moved to Clint's side and quickly knelt down with concern etched deeply on his face.

'Where'd he get you, boy?' Jeff asked anxiously as he started unbuttoning Clint's shirt.

Suddenly another figure was beside him. Tears flowing freely down her freckled cheeks, her red hair brushed Clint's neck and shoulder as Mary hugged him, covering him closer than a saddle blanket.

'Hey!' Clint protested weakly. 'You're both smothering me.' Then he tried to sit up.

Finally managing to get himself free of Mary's petticoats and the kindly ministrations of her and Jeff, Clint got shakily to his feet. A quick check revealed that Silk's bullet had smashed the butt of the revolver he'd taken from Bert Turner, and had ricocheted upward, tearing a long gash across his ribs, but hardly drawing blood.

Although Mary and Jeff were both weak with relief, Mary couldn't refrain from giving Clint a burst of her fiery temper.

'A fine thing you did, Mr. Jefferson Clinton Jackson, worrying Uncle Jeff and me like that, and you with hardly a scratch to show for it,' she said hotly.

Clint had seen how she had shed tears for him and knew how deep her feelings were. Watching her sparkling green eyes, he replied softly: 'Well, missy, would you rather he had killed me?'

'Oh Clint! I was worried sick when I saw you fall,' she wailed and was instantly in his arms, clasping him tightly, and not caring that the whole town was looking on.

Jeff snorted, then turned to retrieve his rifle from the street and began reloading it. He knew that everything would be all right now, as he had seen the light in Clint's eyes when he saw how much the girl cared for him.

Just then, a small party of riders galloped down the street and pulled their lathered horses to a stop before the group. Clint could tell from the set expression on Will Claymore's face that he knew about what had happened to Shirley that morning. He looked from Will to his brother, Paul, then at the other four riders.

'Where is that polecat?' Will demanded in anger, his hand resting on the heavy gun on his hip.

Clint stepped forward with Mary by his side, and said quietly: 'Will, he's dead and it's all over.'

'Where's Neyland?' He asked viciously. 'I want Cole Neyland along with the skunk Barrister, and all the rest of the slimy snakes that worked for him.'

'Will, is that what it took for you to see

what needed to be done?' Clint asked scornfully. 'It seems that something has to strike you pretty close to home for you to act. But, it's finished now. Both Barrister and Neyland are dead.'

'Jackson, it's just started,' Paul Claymore spoke up. 'There's a whole passel of these skunks that needs their necks stretched.'

Clint realized that the situation was liable to turn into a blood bath, so he said quietly: 'Will, you talked to me last night 'bout law and order. Is this your idea of it?'

'We ain't got no law in Pine Creek,' Will reminded him coldly.

'You talked 'bout a badge once,' Clint said evenly. 'Is the offer still open?'

'You ready to clean out this nest of snakes?' Will asked.

'Yep, if'n I can do it my way.'

'All right Clint, the job's yours. You can deputize us right now and we will get started with the hangings.'

'Nope!' Clint replied firmly. 'The first thin' you and these men can do is ride home and let the law handle everythin'. I don't need but one deputy and that's my uncle. Now, all of you ride out a'fore you get on my bad side and I throw you in the hoosegow for disturbin' the peace.'

This statement was met by a few good guffaws, as it was well known that Pine Creek had neither a jail nor a courthouse.

'All right Clint,' Will said. Then, reaching into his pocket, he removed a large oilskin wallet and withdrew a shiny star. 'I've carried this for seven months and waited for the right man to wear it. Can't think of a better man, can you, Paul?' he asked, turning to his younger brother.

'Nope, I'm satisfied.'

Clint hefted the silver star for a moment, then Mary snatched it out of his hand and pinned it to his shirt.

'There!' she said with a toss of her head and a light cheer went up from most of the miners.

'Okay boys, get on home and let the law take care of matters in Pine Creek,' Clint said, and added, 'Will, have a couple of your men go by that cabin up there and brin' in Cole's body. If'n the other man is still there, I want him too.'

'All right Sheriff,' Will replied and the riders reined their horses around and rode out of town.

Looking at the faces about him for a minute, Clint's eyes lingered on the fat, greasy owner of Joe's place. Then Clint said evenly: 'Mister, you got 'til mornin' to clear out. After that, your meat is paid for.'

'You can't run me outta town,' the fat man protested.

'Run or be carried, it's up to you,' he replied. 'Be gone by mornin' or be carryin' iron the next time I see you. Understand, fat man?' Clint warned.

Turning to Mary, he slipped his arm around her tiny waist and said softly: 'Missy, will you give a shot-up man a hand?'

'I'd give him more than that if he asked me right,' she replied with a smile.

'I got a feelin' you might be gettin' asked soon's we can find a preacher to say the words,' Clint said.

Then, together, with Jeff and Moses following, they walked up the street toward the livery stables.

Photoset, printed and bound in Great Britain by REDWOOD BURN LIMITED, Trowbridge, Wiltshire